"Rem_____ _____ _____ring the drinki___ ___e." Micah asked, noticing a cute little brown freckle on her nose that he hadn't seen before.

"During Never Have I Ever?" she asked breathlessly.

"Yes," he said. "Don't think, just do."

She searched his eyes before dropping her gaze to his lips. She leaned in a couple more centimeters.

That's close enough, Micah thought as he crashed his lips to hers. He expected her to be surprised, but instead, her hands went around his neck as she softly moaned into his mouth. She tasted just like he'd imagined she would…sweet and tangy with a hint of wine and tequila from the game they'd been playing.

He probed her mouth open even further and slipped his tongue deeper inside when she parted her lips more. She moaned softly into his mouth and gripped his neck even tighter, lightly massaging the back of his head as she did so. The seductive way she moved her hands just made him want to kiss her harder… longer…until they were both breathless and craving for oxygen. What was it about this woman that pushed him to the brink of insanity? He'd never been this intrigued by a woman before, nor had he enjoyed a kiss quite like this.

Books by Sherelle Green

Harlequin Kimani Romance

A Tempting Proposal
If Only for Tonight
Red Velvet Kisses

SHERELLE GREEN

is a Chicago native with a dynamic imagination and a passion for reading and writing. As a young girl, she channeled her creativity and turned her thoughts into short stories and poems. Although she loves to read all genres, romance holds a special place in her heart. Her love for romance developed in high school after stumbling across a hot and steamy Harlequin novel. She instantly became an avid romance reader and decided to pursue an education in English and journalism. Nothing satisfies her more than writing stories filled with compelling love affairs, multifaceted characters and intriguing relationships. A true romantic, she believes in predestined romances, love at first sight and fairy-tale endings.

Red Velvet kisses

Sherelle Green

H HARLEQUIN® KIMANI™ ROMANCE

To my husband, Henry, for your unconditional love and support. Through the years of our relationship, you have continued to encourage and uplift me. When we first met, I knew you would be an important person in my life, and now that we're embarking on a new future, I'm so excited to continue our journey together. Thank you for being my rock…my strength…and my once in a lifetime love!

Recycling programs for this product may not exist in your area.

ISBN-13: 978-0-373-86379-2

Red Velvet Kisses

Copyright © 2014 by Sherelle Green

For questions and comments about the quality of this book please contact us at CustomerService@Harlequin.com.

HARLEQUIN®
www.Harlequin.com

Printed in U.S.A.

Dear Reader,

Meet vibrant and unique Lexus Turner, co-founder of Elite Events Inc.

Sometimes we are harder on ourselves for the decisions we've made in the past than others are. This deems true for Lex, a woman who has allowed her past mistakes to impact her future. A woman like Lex needs a bad boy like Micah Madden to teach her how to break a few rules. In exchange, Lex offers Micah a love unlike any he's ever had. As the saying goes, opposites attract! And in this case, the attraction is electrifyingly satisfying.

Mya Winters's story is up next, and I can't wait for readers to learn more about her and the hero determined to win her heart. I love to hear from readers, so please feel free to contact me and check out my website for my latest book updates.

Much Love,

Sherelle

www.SherelleGreen.com
AuthorSherelleGreen@gmail.com
@SherelleGreen

To my cousin, Shenelle, for your advice and constant encouragement. When we get together, there's never a dull moment, and it's been that way ever since we were kids. Your comic impersonations, spirited personality and infectious smile bring joy to others. You're so easy to get along with, but there's more to you than meets the eye. In order for people to truly get to know you and see what's inside your heart, they must take the time to peel back the layers of your personality, to find the treasures that lie beneath. You have such passion for delicious dishes, and I love your unique and warm demeanor. When I was thinking about the qualities that I wanted Lex to have, you were definitely my muse. Thanks so much for all the inspiration!

Prologue

"To buy or not to buy," Lexus Turner said to herself
as she admired the pleated lilac babydoll in her hand.
She'd been in Bare Sophistication lingerie boutique for
over thirty minutes and had yet to find something sexy
to purchase. Earlier that morning, she had listened to an
audiobook of a female motivational speaker who stressed
the importance of feeling and looking good. Lexus didn't
have a special someone in her life, but she was tired of
the frumpy, yet comfortable, undies she often wore.

Would this even cover anything? she thought to herself as she observed the uncomfortable-looking tiny silk
thong that accompanied the babydoll. She then pulled
out the silk G-string placed next to the thong. *Now this I
like.* She may have been contradicting herself by dislik-
ing the thong yet liking the G-string, but to her there was
a big difference. The couple times she'd worn a G-string,

she felt as if she was wearing nothing at all. The one and only day she wore a thong, she'd felt as if something was stuck between her butt cheeks all day. That feeling had caused her to not-so-discreetly adjust herself by shaking her leg as she walked.

She looked through the rack at the other lilac panty options. "Oh, now this is different," she said as she held up a panty with a slit in the middle for easy access to her feminine treasures. She could only imagine all the naughty things one could do in a silky lace boyshort with a slit in the center of the panty. It was attached by intertwining ribbons on each side adding to her visual imagination.

"Oh, yes, I love this," she said aloud as she paired the silky lace boyshort with the pleated lilac babydoll. "Perfect match."

"I think you settled on a great set," a deep voice said behind her. Startled, Lexus turned around quicker than anticipated, running right into the solid chest of the man with the low timbre voice. She jumped back from the intensity of the direct contact and misjudged her steps. The oversight of the large rack caused her to trip over her feet and sent her tumbling right into a pair of powerful bronzed arms.

"I'm sorry, I didn't mean to startle you," he said as he helped her regain her balance.

Lexus tried to speak, but she couldn't formulate any words. *Oh...my...goodness.* The man looked tastier than the tiramisu she'd sampled earlier at a local coffee shop. His eyes were chestnut brown with gray specs sprinkled in the coloring. And from what she could tell by the outline of his clothes, he had the body of a god. She was pretty sure she was drooling, which probably didn't look sexy at all.

She tried to stop her eyes from looking him up and down in admiration, but she couldn't help it. He was wearing jeans and a button-up with quarter-length sleeves. He looked slightly familiar and had the sexiest deep dimples she'd ever seen on a man. She couldn't have met him before because she was sure she would have remembered a man this fine.

"Do you need me to help you with that?" he asked.

Lexus squinted her eyes together in confusion until she followed his gaze and noticed that all of the belongings from her purse had fallen out and were scattered across the floor.

"Oh, crap," she whispered as she bent down and began picking everything up. The man bent down to help her, and although Lexus wanted to tell him not to, she still couldn't speak. She'd met attractive men before, but none had left her speechless.

"You sure do have a lot of lipstick," he said with a laugh as he handed her two of the six tubes that had fallen near his feet.

Come on girl! Say something, Lex chanted in her head. Still nothing. Not a single word. Instead, she gave him a big smile and tried to make a sexy *I love lipstick and look good in it* sort of laugh, but it came off as an *I have issues please don't ask me any more questions* type of laugh.

Big fail. *Why do I even try?*

"Would you like me to ring that up for you," he asked as he picked up the lilac babydoll and boyshort that had fallen on the floor, as well. Lexus timidly nodded her head in agreement.

Making her way to the counter, she admired his walk

and the way his butt moved in his jeans. She looked down at her outfit, wishing she'd chosen to wear cute skinny jeans, a flattering top and stylish shoes rather than leggings, a simple T-shirt and gym shoes that needed a good cleaning. She'd just left a nearby workout facility so she was sure the once smooth edges of her hair were now in little curly cues. Her fellow cofounders at Elite Events Incorporated always told her to dress in sexier workout gear, but she never listened. *I should have taken their advice. Or at least worn a headband.*

When they got to the register, he began ringing up her items. She noticed that his eyes lingered on the panties a little more than the babydoll. When he lifted his face back to her he seemed amused. She couldn't tell if he wanted to flirt with her or laugh at her since it seemed she had no business buying such raunchy underwear. The fact that she couldn't tell the difference from the expression on his face was even more unsettling.

"You don't talk much do you?" he asked her as he bagged her items.

"Hahaha, um, yeah. Oh, boy do I." *Huh! What did she just say?* The amused look on his face turned into a hearty laugh. Lexus only felt it fitting to awkwardly laugh along with him although she saw nothing funny about her current situation.

"You're adorable," he said as he handed her the receipt. *Adorable?* Lexus thought as she raised an eyebrow at the man. She definitely didn't want the hot guy thinking about her as *adorable, cute* or any other word best used to describe a bunny, *not* a woman he found attractive. She had to hightail it out of there before she embarrassed herself any further.

Grabbing her bag, she flashed him a small smile before turning to the door. She arrived at the front entrance of the boutique just as a woman was entering. "Thanks so much sweetie," the woman said as she hastily made her way to the man that had helped her and gave him a tight hug. "You're the best," she continued as she gave him a kiss on the cheek.

Oh, well...you win some, you lose some. And there was no doubt in her mind that she wasn't winning this man even before his girlfriend walked into the shop.

When Lexus stepped outside, the hot August air did nothing to calm the inferno the man inside the shop had ignited within her. She hastily walked to the edge of the block before rounding the corner. Briefly stopping to lean on a nearby wall, she took a couple minutes to think about the recent course of events. The motivational audiobook she had studied said that she should take charge of her life and be aggressive. Well, she definitely hadn't taken charge of that situation. And even though she didn't have an aggressive bone in her body, she'd wished she had at least tried to be the aggressor back in the lingerie shop.

"It doesn't matter. He has a girlfriend anyway," she reminded herself as she thought about the exchange between him and the woman who entered the store when she was leaving.

Getting up from the wall, Lexus put her headphones back in and began listening to the motivational audiobook she'd downloaded through iTunes. She only had a couple hours to get ready before her business partner and cousin Cydney Rayne's dinner party in the Chicago River North area. Cyd had just gotten back from a weeklong vacation in Anguilla with her boyfriend, Shawn Miles.

As she walked back to her condo the words coming through her headphones almost made her want to cut off her phone completely. "You are in control of your own destiny. You can be the aggressor. In order to love someone else, you have to love yourself. There is nothing wrong with a vocal woman. You can do it. Just give it a try."

Lexus blew out a frustrated breath as she continued to listen to the voice coming from her headphones. "Yeah, yeah…be the aggressor. I got it," she huffed aloud.

Lex hopped off the CTA Red Line train and glanced at her cell phone. She was rarely late, but the glass of red wine she'd had after returning home from the lingerie shop had caused her to fall asleep. When she woke up, she'd realized she only had thirty minutes before the dinner started.

"Hello, I'm here for the Cydney Rayne dinner party," she said to the hostess when she arrived at the restaurant.

"Right this way miss." Lex followed the woman to the private room. After apologizing for her tardiness, she gave hugs to everyone in attendance including her other two Elite Events business partners, Imani Rayne-Barker and Mya Winters. She took one of the two vacant seats at the end of the dinner table when Cyd's boyfriend, Shawn, tapped his fork on his wineglass.

"Now that almost everyone is here, we have an announcement to make," Shawn said.

"Shawn and I are engaged!" Cyd finished as she stuck out her hand to reveal a gorgeous three-carat diamond ring.

"Oh, my gosh, congratulations!" Lex exclaimed as she jumped from her seat and rushed over to hug Cyd, followed by others offering their congrats.

"I guess I missed something," said a familiar baritone

voice from the doorway of the room. *What the heck is he doing here?*

"Everyone," Shawn said gathering the attention from the group and making his way to the man. "This is one of my best friends and my business partner, Micah Madden. He just moved to Chicago last month and if he accepts, he will be my best man."

Lex watched with eyes wide open as the two men embraced while Micah shared his congrats. She barely heard Cyd's story of how Shawn proposed in Anguilla because she was too busy staring at Micah, hoping that he wasn't the same person she thought he was.

Unless he has a twin, that's definitely him. As if he knew she was analyzing him, his eyes landed on her and slowly looked her up and down before he began walking toward her. She had to get out of there.

"I'll be right back," she said to the group of women, although they were too busy listening to Cyd's story to hear her. She turned and walked around the table in the opposite direction Micah was walking.

Once she was in the hallway, she slipped into a nearby bathroom and took a deep breath. *He's just a man. A normal man.* She glanced at her reflection in the mirror. Who was she kidding? He wasn't a normal man. He was a fine man. A tempting man. A man with a nice round butt begging to be grabbed. Lex was a sucker for a man with a nice butt. *And why the heck am I just meeting him!* Shawn and Cyd had been dating for eight months. She didn't remember Micah at any of Shawn's previous get-togethers since he hadn't lived in Chicago. But she definitely knew his name. Both Cyd and Shawn had mentioned him on more than one occasion.

Last year, Cyd had planned a series of appreciation

events for the Peter Vallant Company and had gotten kidnapped at the winter formal. Shawn and Micah had been securing the series of events and Shawn had saved Cyd from a crazy woman who'd become obsessed with her. Micah had been at the formal, but Lex hadn't arrived until after he was assigned to watch Cyd so their paths had never crossed that night. If she hadn't had another event that day, she probably could have met him that night and saved herself some embarrassment. Usually, when Lex met an extremely attractive man for the first time, she performed a ritual to help settle her nerves. The ritual started with a quick pep talk in the mirror similar to the one she was giving herself now and it ended with a conversation with Mya who often gave her witty things to say so she could keep the guy on his toes. An unprepared Lex equaled embarrassment and she had already been embarrassed enough for one day.

"Okay girl," she said to herself. "You can't hide in here forever." Fluffing her curls and reapplying a coat of red lipstick, she exited the bathroom, running right into a solid chest. Caught off guard, she tripped over his feet and twirled around so suddenly that she sent them both tumbling to the ground.

"Ouch," she said, landing hard on the man. When she heard him let out a loud groan, she looked up at his face. *Oh, great.*

"I'm sorry," she said as she attempted to get off of him.

"We have got to stop meeting like this, lingerie girl," Micah said, not easing his grip on her. *Lingerie girl... that's kinda cute.* Unfortunately, the way her purple summer dress was gathered high on her thighs was not cute at all. She was sure a part of her panties were showing.

"Can you let me go now?" she asked as she struggled

out of his arms. He finally let her go. When she stood, she nervously glanced around to see how many people were around to witness their fall.

"You're so adorable," he said to her before taking a step forward.

Here we go with this word again. She took a step back. "I'm sure you say that to your girlfriend, too." *Real subtle Lex.*

"What girlfriend?"

"The one who kissed you on the cheek in the lingerie shop today."

"That woman was my cousin, Winter Dupree," Micah said with a laugh. "She owns Bare Sophistication lingerie boutique and she needed me to watch the store for a few hours. The store just opened and she doesn't have much staff right now."

Cousin? Just kill me know. "And on that embarrassing note, I think I'll go back to join the group," she said leaving him in the hallway.

"Don't turn around. Just keep walking," she said to herself. But even with the warning, she had to know if he was staring at her. When she reached the end of the hallway, she slightly turned her head. Micah was still standing there with his hands in his pockets and a sly smile on his face. He looked handsome. And downright dangerous. *Mercy.*

Chapter 1

Three months later...

Lexus Turner stared out of her window seat on the CTA bus as she admired the holiday shops and boutiques festively decorated along the Magnificent Mile. She loved living in downtown Chicago, but driving in traffic often made her nervous, so she opted to take public transportation instead. Doing so allowed her the opportunity to admire her beautiful city and embark on some of the best festivities Chicago had to offer.

Lexus completely ignored the loud hustle and bustle of Chicagoans getting on and off the bus as they made their way through downtown for an array of winter festivities. When she reached her stop, she stepped off the bus and breathed in the crisp November air. Soft flakes were beginning to fall and the loud salt trucks caused a few pedestrians to take cover under store awnings to avoid the swinging salt from the trucks' brushes. Some people disliked the busyness of the city, but Lexus loved the constant activity and noisy atmosphere.

As she made her way into the tall skyscraper and arrived on the floor where her company was located, she admired the new logo that was intricately painted on the main office glass door. When Lexus, Imani, Cyd and Mya had joined forces and founded Elite Events Incorporated, they could have never predicted their company would take off so fast. They each ran their respective divisions while alternating as lead planner on each event the company booked. Lexus considered herself lucky to be able to run a successful business with those closest to her.

"Good morning, Ellie," Lexus said to the office assistant as she began removing her snow-white scarf and jet-black peacoat.

"Good morning, Miss Turner."

Before she made it completely through the second glass door that separated the lounge from the main office, Cyd met her halfway.

"Lex! Great, you're finally here," Cyd said as she led her through the hall to the back of the floor where the conference rooms were located.

"Why the rush, Cyd?" she asked with a smile as her warm brown curls bounced around her shoulders.

"Well, we need to decide who will lead a 35th anniversary party that Micah Madden wants to have for his parents. He has a meeting down the street so he dropped by the office a few minutes ago. Mya told him we could all meet with him before he leaves for his own meeting," Cyd explained.

The smile fell from Lex's smooth caramel face the instant she heard that Micah was in the office.

"Judging by the look on your face, that's exactly how I thought you would feel," Cyd said with a giggle. "That's why I came out of the room to warn you."

Three months ago Shawn proposed to Cyd and she happily accepted. The two were getting married next summer and Lex and Micah were both in the wedding party. Unfortunately for Lex, that meant she would be seeing a lot more of Micah as the wedding grew closer.

"A meeting? How convenient. Seriously, Cyd, I don't even understand why he has to plan a 35th anniversary party for his parents anyway. Why not plan a 40th anniversary party like any other normal person."

"Actually, the percentage rate for people who have 35th anniversary parties is very high and increasing every year," Micah said, standing behind Lex and Cyd. "My parents have never had a grand anniversary party so I think it's long overdue."

Crap, what are the odds, Lex thought to herself as she dropped her head to the floor. *Of course he's standing right behind me.* The man always had a way of sneaking up on her.

"I wasn't trying to sneak up on you," Micah stated, sensing her thoughts. "I had to step into the hallway to take an important phone call."

Lex recovered from her embarrassment and lifted her head before turning around to face Micah.

"Hello, Lexus Turner," Micah said as he extended his hand to greet her. There he was…in the flesh. The one man she wished didn't occupy so many of her thoughts. Most people called her Lex instead of Lexus, but her full name rolled off his tongue as if he said her name every day. Better yet, by the deepness in his voice, you'd think he said her name every night.

"Hello, Micah Madden," Lex said, taking her cue from him and saying his full name, as well. "It's good to see you again."

Micah stood there observing her, his eyes burning a hole through her snug-fitting sweater dress. When his eyes left her dress and reached her lips, they lingered there for a while. On instinct, she licked her rosy colored lips trying to stop the pulsating feeling between her legs. Every time she was near him, she couldn't help but be consumed by his presence. The first quality she studied on him today were his muscular arms that were clearly visible through his white fitted dress shirt. The second quality she observed were his perfect white teeth and sexy dimpled smile. The third quality she liked was his unique sense of style. The man could wear a pair of sleek slacks and slim black tie like no other, and always looked as if he'd just walked off the runway.

"Likewise," Micah finally replied as he finished appraising her. "You look very nice today LG." She wished she knew why he thought it was okay to call her LG. He had started calling her LG two and a half months ago at Cyd and Shawn's official engagement party. It was short for lingerie girl. No one knew what it meant except for the two of them and when anyone asked, she never told them. He always called her LG after initially greeting her as Lexus. *What is with this guy?* If she ever got the nerve, she would question him about it. She wanted to question him now, but she couldn't. Secretly, she liked the way it made her feel. Even saying the nickname he'd given her, Lex thought he made it sound heavenly.

Cyd cleared her throat.

"Oh, and you look very nice as well, Cyd," Micah replied.

"Why, thanks," Cyd said as she flipped her jet-black hair over her shoulders. "It's so nice of you to finally notice that I'm standing here. I was about to tell you both to take it to the bedroom."

"Cyd!" Lex exclaimed loudly. "Really?"

"No, she's right," Micah interjected. "We should handle this." At Lex's raised eyebrow he continued. "I meant that we should get started with the meeting. I wasn't referring to the bedroom comment."

Lex breathed a sigh of relief.

"Unless there's something you want to tell me," Micah stated aloud, looking solely at Lex.

"Nope, nothing to tell," she responded a little too quickly.

"You two are hard to watch," Cyd said as she shook her head and glanced from Lex to Micah. "Let's just go into the conference room. Imani and Mya are waiting."

While Micah and Cyd were making themselves comfortable at the conference table, Lex decided to pour a much-needed cup of coffee. She took her seat next to Imani, but not before she cut Cyd a slicing look of irritation.

Cyd responded to the look by innocently lifting her hands and eyebrows in indication that she didn't understand what Lex was referring to.

"Ha! Yeah, right," Lex said aloud, although she hadn't intended to.

"Is everything okay?" Imani asked.

"Yup, everything is fine," Lex replied. *As long as I keep my hormones in check.*

"Great! Now let's get down to business. As you all

know, Micah would like to throw a 35th anniversary party for his parents in their Arkansas hometown. First things first, we need to decide who will lead this event."

"I think Lex should handle this event," Mya quickly replied.

"I agree," Cyd added.

"Sounds good to me," Imani continued after Cyd.

"Great. Then, it's settled," Micah said as he stood to shake each woman's hand before finally reaching Lex.

"I have to get to work. But let's set a date to meet and discuss my needs."

Lex was a little taken aback by his comment and the fact that her partners had decided she would be the event lead. Micah was still holding her hand when he voiced the last words. *Did he mean work needs or personal needs?*

"Both," Micah said as if reading her thoughts again.

"I'm sorry, what did you say?" Lex asked in confusion. Everything was happening too fast and she couldn't react that quickly. "Never mind, I will call you to set up a preliminary meeting for the anniversary party. Is there any day this week that doesn't work well for you?"

Micah finally let go of her hand and flashed another priceless smile.

"Any day this week works for me." He winked, clearly entertained by the fact that, once again, she was ignoring his advances. With that, he gave a quick nod to all the women and left the conference room.

"What just happened here?" Lex asked Mya in particular after Micah was out of earshot. "Last week, I thought we both agreed that we would figure out what Micah wanted for the anniversary party before deciding who would be the best planner since Imani and Cyd already have a few events lined up."

"I don't remember us saying that," Mya responded as she pretended to be occupied with straightening a stack of unruly papers. "I talked to Micah when he first got here so I already knew that it worked best with your schedule."

Imani and Cyd both laughed. While eyeing her friends and partners, Lex tried to figure out exactly what scheme they were trying to get away with.

"I'm pretty sure that's what we discussed," Lex said raising her voice a bit. "And what do you mean it worked best with my schedule. He didn't even say what date he was interested in so you couldn't possibly know what worked best."

"Yes, he did," Mya answered. "His parents never had a real wedding, but their actual wedding date is Valentine's Day. He said that he wanted to plan their anniversary sometime next month before New Years, or after if that's too soon. Like I said, I'd already talked to him."

"That soon?" Lex exclaimed. "Why did we agree to plan this party? It's already November!"

"We've planned plenty of parties with way less time," Imani responded. "Besides, you still have another two weeks left in this month."

"And let's not forget that last year, I planned the formal for the Peter Vallant Company with way less time than you have," Cyd added. "I had about two weeks to plan that entire event. If I can make that work, you can definitely make this work."

Lex crossed her arms over her chest in annoyance. Her body language was a clear indication that she was pouting, but she didn't care. She felt as if she was the focal point of the joke, and being the main focus of any joke was *not* a good feeling.

Mya's smartphone vibrated. "Lex, I'd love to continue this conversation but I have to meet with a client to discuss the grand opening event for their new clothing store."

"Of course you do," Lex said sarcastically. Imani and Cyd had their phones in their hands as well, and if Lex was a betting woman, she'd bet any dollar amount that one of them had texted Mya to give her an excuse to leave the conference room.

"I have to go, too," Imani stated. "I have to tweet about a couple upcoming events and I have to update our page on Facebook."

"I should probably call the florist for my wedding to confirm my appointment next week," Cyd interjected. "Besides, I'm sure you have to start working on a game plan for the anniversary party."

"Ugh," Lex responded in annoyance. "I know what you guys are doing and it won't work."

"Sweetie, that childlike pout doesn't look good on you," Cyd said with a laugh.

"Besides, we don't know what you're talking about," Mya added.

"Oh, really," Lex said sitting upright in her chair while uncrossing her arms and bracing both hands on the conference table.

"Look, I'm not blind. I know Micah has a thing for me. But y'all know I'm not going there with a man like him."

"Lex, listen to yourself," Cyd said. "Micah is educated, successful and sexy. Plus he's a bit of a bad boy. Trust me, women in Chicago have been drooling all over him ever since he moved here this past summer."

"But he's only interested in you," Imani added.

Rubbing her hands over her face, Lex tried to ignore what they were saying. She couldn't date a man like him.

He was too easy to fall for and after everything she'd been through, she wasn't willing to risk her heart again.

"You guys know what I went through with Evan."

Imani reached over and softly touched Lex's hand. "Lex, we all know that Evan's craziness made you swear off men. But you can't let him define your future. You need to move on from that situation."

"I know," Lex replied. "But it's not that easy. He controlled every part of me in high school and college. If I hadn't seen the light after Gamine's death, I would have never realized the type of man he was." When her grandmother, Faith Gamine Burrstone died a few years ago, a light switch had finally been turned on in Lex's head.

"Sweetie, Evan Gilmore was the ultimate a-hole!" Cyd exclaimed. "We all blame ourselves for not always speaking up when it came to our true thoughts about him. But Micah Madden is not Evan Gilmore."

"Not even close," Mya added. "You're twenty-eight. You need to date a real man."

"I have dated real men," Lex said, defending herself. "Remember Reginald Collins?"

"Right, how can we forget nerdy Reginald," Cyd cynically replied. "I still don't understand why you wasted your time on someone who didn't even like to kiss in public…or private I presume."

"That's not true," Lex responded. "He was just very selective on how and when he showed his feelings." She wouldn't dare tell them that even though they'd dated for over seven months, they hadn't had sex and had barely even kissed.

"A peck on the cheek is not a kiss," Imani stated. "And that's all we ever saw him give you…a light peck on the cheek. Even with that peck, he did it sloppily."

"He sure did," Mya agreed. "It made us gag just watching it. Like he wanted to open his mouth and French kiss your cheek, but decided against it. Awkward."

"Okay," Lex said drawling out the word. "Enough about my last boyfriend."

"If you can even call him that," Cyd mumbled beneath her breath.

"Anyway," Lex continued, "since I don't have a choice, I will plan the anniversary party. But I want to make it clear that I will continue to look at Micah in a completely professional manner."

"Hmm, and how is that working out for you so far?" Mya said, laughing. Imani and Cyd followed suit and joined in the laughter.

"Oh, you guys didn't see them in the hall earlier," Cyd said, ready to spill all the juicy details.

"Oh, do tell," Imani said, rubbing her hands together.

"My work can wait," Mya said, making no attempts to leave the room as she'd previously been prepared to do.

"Well I don't think I need to stay around for this," Lex said as she gathered her stuff and walked out of the conference room. Before the door fully closed, she heard the women giggle as Cyd explained how she'd made the situation even more awkward for her and Micah when she had suggested that they take it to the bedroom.

Chapter 2

When Lex got to her office, she quickly shut and locked the door. Slipping off her winter boots and replacing them with her ballerina flats, she took a seat in her cozy chair behind her large mahogany desk. She then twirled in the seat until she was facing her window with a partial view of Lake Michigan.

"I knew I should have called in sick today," Lex said to herself. It probably wouldn't have even mattered. Micah Madden had been a constant distraction to her stable psyche since she'd met him in the lingerie shop.

"Lord, give me strength," she said as she shook her head and softly closed her eyes. She needed to avoid his advances and treat him like any other client. Otherwise, she had no doubt that she'd lose herself in him.

A soft knock on her door interrupted her thoughts. "Coming," Lex said loudly for the person on the other side of the door to hear. As soon as she opened the door, she wished she'd first asked who was behind the closed door before crossing the room.

"Yes, Micah?" she asked with more disdain in her voice than she'd intended.

"Well, I'm happy to see you, too, Lex," he said, his filled with laughter.

She stood back to let him enter her office. "I thought you left," she said, making sure her behind swayed when she walked back to her desk.

"I was almost out the building when I remembered that I needed to give you a few notes I had about my parents. You know, their likes, dislikes…that sort of thing. That way, you can start planning now if you'd like." He reached out his hand to give her a typed sheet of paper.

As Lex took the paper, she made sure their hands didn't touch. The last thing she needed was any close contact. She glanced up at him again. Their chemistry was undeniable and it seemed the more she saw him the harder it was to ignore how badly her body wanted him. Her mind was saying, *Heck no, you better stay away.* But her body was screaming, *Girl, what in the world is wrong with you? Sleep with him already!*

Lex cleared her throat and briefly looked at the paper again. When she looked back up to Micah, he glanced from the paper she was holding to her eyes and flashed one of his infamous half smiles. He had to know she was daydreaming about him. He was a smart man and probably felt the heat emanating from their bodies just as strongly as she could.

"Well, I guess I'll be going then," Micah stated as he turned to leave her office. Lex followed, heading to the door so that she could lock it behind him. She didn't need any more interruptions until the afternoon. When he reached the door, he quickly turned to face her, completely catching Lex off guard and causing her to run directly into his chest.

"Why do you always do that," Lex squealed as she tried to back away from him. But she couldn't. Her feet wouldn't move the second she gazed into his piercing eyes. He began taking deep breaths, his eyes slowly dragging over her entire body. Lex couldn't breathe. She feared that he would make a move if she so much as batted an eyelash. She wasn't sure how long they stood there before he finally said something.

"You can't fight it for much longer."

Just watch me. "I don't know what you mean," Lex said, deciding to play stupid. Micah stepped a little closer to her, further invading her personal space.

"Sooner or later, I will have you positioned spread-eagle style on my bed."

"I should smack you for saying that," she quickly replied, surprised by his blunt comment.

"But you won't," he responded, getting even closer to her. "You wouldn't hurt me."

"You don't know what I'd do," Lex replied, trying to sound as sassy as she could under the circumstances.

"Yes, I do," Micah said. "But that's not all I want to do to you."

Lex squinted her eyes. She shouldn't ask him to go on, but she was way too curious to end the conversation there. "What else do you want to do to me?"

Micah glanced at her lips before looking back into her eyes. "You'll see soon enough."

Concluding that he wasn't saying anything more, she finally exhaled. Her eyes dropped to his lips before she could stop them. She positioned her foot so that she could take a step back from him, but he moved toward her again, stalling her in her place.

"Be careful LG," he said as he took one finger and dragged it over her lips. "I'm usually not a patient man so your time avoiding me is almost up." She gasped out of surprise, but didn't move away from his touch. Her gasp gave him the opportunity to slightly dip his finger into her mouth. He then took his lipstick-smeared finger into his mouth and gently sucked the tip.

"I can only imagine how good you really taste," he said before taking another long look at her lips.

"Ew, I don't know where your hands have been," she stated as she took a step back from him. She huffed aloud, irritated at herself for not initially smacking his hand away, and aggravated at her mouth for wanting to suck his finger longer.

"Maybe not," he said as he moved closer again, this time bringing his face close to her ear. "But I can tell you where my hands want to go."

Once again, she gasped. Lex tried to think of a comeback, but her mind was blank, replaced by a feeling that was becoming all too familiar when she was around Micah Madden.

"See you soon," he said as he walked out her door. Once he was gone, she leaned against her closed door and chastised herself for not being stronger.

"How in the world am I going to plan this anniversary party?" she asked herself. She had too much baggage and she needed a safe guy…a predictable guy. *Not* the type who represented every wet fantasy rolled into one hot male specimen.

Walking away from the closed door, she went back to her desk in hopes that Micah wouldn't invade her dreams later.

Micah twirled his keys around his finger as he made his way to his parked Mercedes-Benz. Micah and Shawn had finally decided to name their security firm M&M Security and headquarter the company in Chicago. After leaving the police force, Micah had wanted a new start so he didn't mind where the company was located. And after he had met Lex, he'd been even more satisfied with the location. He wanted Lex in the worst way possible and his needs went way beyond the bedroom.

Sliding into his leather seat, he pulled out of the circular parking garage and into Chicago's morning traffic. He hadn't lied about his meeting. He had to meet with a potential investor in the security firm in two hours. But first, he had to meet with Shawn to discuss a few details.

Although he'd only been in Chicago for six months, he had grown quite fond of the city. Leaving his job as a police officer in Arkansas had been the best decision he could have made. He enjoyed being in business for himself and he knew he had to leave the police force after realizing that it was way more corrupt than he could have ever imagined.

He turned off of Michigan Ave. onto a side street, minutes away from the M&M Security office. His thoughts instantly returned to Lex. When he'd arrived in Chicago over the summer, he was glad he could check on his cousin and see how her new lingerie boutique was doing. He had hoped that a woman would catch his eye, but he definitely wasn't prepared to meet Lexus Turner. He hated to sound shallow, but Lex was not the type of woman he was usually attracted to. Lex was the type of woman you wife and he was more accustomed to dating the type of woman you simply bed.

Her natural beauty had captured him from the moment he first saw her. And her clumsiness and failure to form a complete sentence around him had only intrigued him more. He couldn't explain why he was so fascinated by a woman who'd made it clear that she wanted nothing to do with him. Gone was the unsure, wide-eyed woman he'd met in the lingerie shop. She'd been replaced by a woman who avoided his advances every chance she got and she wasn't afraid to tell him no.

Micah turned up his radio and instantly, Jay-Z's latest hit filled the car's speakers. Pulling up to a stop sign, he delayed at the sign to let three women cross the street. They took their sweet time walking, too busy flirtatiously looking at him through the front glass of the car. The one with the tight jeans, boot heels and slim winter coat caught his eye. When she turned around, Micah noticed that she was the same woman who had approached him several times at a bar near his office. Micah flashed her a smile and she waved just before stopping at the corner of the sidewalk and crooking her finger to indicate that she wanted him to pull over. *Flirting with other women will definitely get my mind off Lex.*

He pulled over as directed and watched the woman seductively walk in his direction. *Lex would look better in those jeans,* he thought. Micah shook his head, annoyed that even a woman as attractive as the one walking toward his car could not take his mind off Lex.

"Where are you headed to?" the woman voiced as she leaned over his car window, licking her lips in a way he assumed was supposed to be attractive.

"I'm headed to work," he replied with a smile.

"I live right around the corner. Do you have some time to spare?"

The smile began to fade from Micah's face. *This is what you pulled over for...right?* "In fact, I'm already late so I should go," he continued, brushing her off. She took the hint and stood up from his car window.

"Why did you even pull over?" she huffed with an irritated frown.

"My mistake," he said as he gave her a slight wave and took off. *Crap.* It wasn't like him to be so into a woman who wouldn't even give him the time of day. He knew Lex was attracted to him, but he didn't understand why she spent so much time ignoring his advances when she could clearly feel the chemistry. On several occasions when they were out with their friends, Micah would catch Lex staring at him with wistful eyes full of lust. He wasn't extremely cocky, but he knew he was a damn good catch, and women—like the one he just left— had been throwing themselves at him since he'd arrived in Chicago. All except for the one woman who he craved more than he had ever desired any woman.

When he arrived at M&M Security he greeted the receptionist before making his way to Shawn's office and knocking on the door.

"Come in," Shawn announced. Micah walked in and sat down in a nearby chair.

"What's wrong?" Shawn asked, reading the tense look on his face.

"Man, I'm only gonna tell you this because I know you've been there," Micah said as he let out a frustrated huff of air. Shawn laughed as if he already knew where the conversation was headed.

"Does this have to do with Lex?"

"Of course it has to do with her," Micah exclaimed. "I had a meeting with all the ladies this morning and within minutes, Lex was informed that she would be the event planner for my parents' anniversary party."

"Isn't that a good thing?"

"It is, but it's what happened after I left the office that caught me off guard."

"What happened?"

Micah dragged his long fingers across his face. "Remember that woman from the bar the other night? The one who wore those blue stilettos and tight jeans? We danced a few times before you and I left."

"Yeah, I remember."

"Well, I ran into her on my way to the office and she invited me back to her place."

"In the middle of the day? Man, some women are bold nowadays," Shawn said shaking his head. "But from the annoyed look on your face, I'm assuming you declined her offer."

"Sure did," Micah said as he dropped his head to the floor.

"So I guess the self-imposed streak of celibacy continues," Shawn said with a laugh.

"You know when I turned thirty this year I promised myself that I would stop sleeping around."

"Sleeping around with so many women, yes. Not sleeping with any women period, no."

"I've been too busy trying to get settled in Chicago to think about having sex with random women. Besides—" Micah glanced out the side window in Shawn's office "—there's only one woman I have my eye on, and until

Lex accepts the inevitable, I don't think I'll be satisfied with any other woman. That sounds crazy, right?"

"Well, considering I know the type of man you used to be, hell, yeah. But I understand," Shawn responded leaning back in his desk chair. "I felt the same way about Cyd, but luckily, Cyd didn't make me wait that long. Plus, I heard that Lex was in a serious relationship for years, one that went terribly wrong. According to Cyd, she's sworn off dating real men."

"So that means what? She dates fake men?"

"I don't know. Cyd and I got distracted so we never finished the conversation."

Micah didn't even bother asking what had distracted Shawn and Cyd since he already knew. Nor did he bother to ask about Lex's old relationships because he'd asked Shawn before and he said he needed to ask Lex. So he would just have to find out from her. There was way more to Lex than met the eye, and he was determined to figure it out. He'd spent the past few months observing her and patiently waiting for her to stop fighting the desire she was trying to hide. Now he was done waiting. Micah never had to persistently pursue a woman, but Lex was making him work for it. But if he left it to her they would never get together, so it was time for him to stop letting Lex control the course of their nonexistent relationship.

"Then I guess I will just have to show Lex that I don't plan on going anywhere."

"And I assume your sudden desire to throw your parents an anniversary party plays a part in your plans?"

"That and the fact that they deserve a celebration," Micah said, rubbing his hands together. "Up until now, I've been giving Lex time to realize that she can't fight the attraction forever. But I think it's time to lay out all the stops the only way a Madden man knows how to."

"I'm afraid to ask," Shawn said with a laugh as he pulled out a folder that contained notes on the investor they were meeting with in an hour. "Well, Romeo, I can't wait to see how this plan of yours plays out. In the meantime, let's get ready for our meeting."

Micah was barely listening to Shawn as he went over the notes in the file. His mind was already racing with different seduction tactics. *Time for you to see things my way, Lex.*

Chapter 3

"Ya'll couldn't possibly expect me to agree to this," Lex shouted as she slammed a piece of paper on Imani's desk. It had only been three days since she'd seen Micah and he was already working her last nerve.

"Let's be reasonable, Lex," Imani said as she stood from her chair and walked around her desk. "If a client needs us to travel we almost always accommodate their needs."

"She's right," Mya said, entering Imani's office with Cyd by her side. "Our main goal at Elite Events Incorporated is to make every event we plan a memorable experience. We achieve this by putting our all into every event we plan."

"Please save the speech for someone who didn't help cofound this company or create part of the mission statement," Lex said as she turned slightly to Mya and raised a hand to cut her off.

"Someone's bitchy this morning," Cyd said as she plopped down in a nearby chair. Lex cut her eyes at Cyd before taking a step back so she could face all the women. She took a couple deep breaths before she continued her rant.

"Look," she stated firmly. "Micah's request that I accompany him to his Arkansas hometown to get to know his parents better should *not* be a requirement."

"How is this any different than when you and I attended several family outings to get to know the families of Kaydence Walters and Justin Phillips before we planned their wedding and prewedding festivities earlier this year?" Mya asked.

"Or when Cyd and I spent three days with the families of Brooklyn Hathaway and Wyatt Lexington for the exact same reason before we began planning their wedding?" Imani interjected.

"All of that didn't require us to leave Chicago. Did any of you actually read this piece of paper before agreeing to his contract?" Lex asked as she picked up the paper from Imani's desk and waved it in the air. "Well let me inform you of Mr. Madden's ridiculous requests."

She flipped some fallen hair out of her face before she gripped the paper with both hands. "Number one—the event planner must meet with me in person once a week to ensure we are on schedule with the plans. Number two—the event planner must agree to at least three dinner meetings as my daily schedule is too busy for morning or afternoon consultations. Number three—the event planner must attend the winter festival in my Arkansas hometown during the month of December."

She placed the piece of paper back on the desk before looking at her partners. The smirks on their faces were really starting to get under her skin. "I don't think anything is funny about this situation!"

"Well, if you were looking at the situation through our eyes, maybe you would," Mya said with a laugh and shrug of her shoulders.

"Oh, lord," Cyd said getting up from the chair. "Lex, we know you're pissed off, but honestly, we've done more for clients before. You're usually so accommodating and you rarely complain so we can only assume that you like Micah more than you have let on."

"Oh, please," Lex said, waving off the comment. "I just value my time and with Christmas right around the corner, it irritates me that Micah is trying to occupy so much of it."

"Or," Imani responded as she placed her pointer finger in the air. "Spending that much time with Micah irritates you because you can't avoid him like you have been lately."

She sighed deeply. Lex was tired of arguing about the same subject and was even more tired of convincing herself they were wrong when she knew, deep down, that they were right. She dropped her head down to the floor before lifting it back up.

"I give up," Lex said taking a seat in the chair Cyd had just vacated. "You guys are right, but I just don't get it. Why is he even into me when he can have his pick of women? I've constantly ignored his advances."

"Do you hear yourself?" Mya asked raising an eyebrow. "Why not you? He'd be lucky to have you."

Lex wasn't so sure. The ladies didn't know how embarrassing it was the first time she'd met him. And once she realized she would have to see him again, she'd decided that she could either be that pathetic woman he met in the lingerie boutique, or she could act indifferent to him, which somehow came off as dislike. That wasn't her intention, but anything was better than being submissive to his charm.

She covered her face with both hands. "I'm done talking about Micah. Like I said before, I have too much baggage to even consider dating a man like him. Besides," she said getting up from the chair and smoothing out her dress slacks. "I've avoided his advances for this long so I'm sure another month or so will be a piece of cake."

"Are you sure about that?"

Lex jumped at the sound of Micah's voice in the doorway. *Oh, no...how much did he hear?* From the sly smile on his smooth brown face she could only assume he'd heard way too much.

"I hate when you do that," she said placing her hands on her hips and glaring at him. The man made her tense, and Lex hated feeling on edge. And why was he just standing there not saying anything? *Fine! If he wants to stand there and stare at me, I can do the same thing.* The only problem with that plan was that Micah had mastered the act of seduction and the thoughts reflected in his eyes made her heart beat ten times faster than normal.

"Your office assistant, Ellie, told me I could go directly into your office. I went there first," Micah finally said.

"Hmm. Funny that she didn't make you wait in the lobby." Lex looked around at her partners knowing that one of them had probably given Ellie the okay to add Micah to the list of people who could stop by without appointments. Otherwise, there was no way he would have been allowed to see her without first calling and scheduling an appointment.

"Can we talk?" he asked, his stare still unwavering. Today he looked more casual in jeans, a black polo and black peacoat. He removed his winter hat and instantly, Lex wished she could run her fingers through his soft natural black curls.

I really wasn't prepared to see him today. "Sure," Lex answered as she walked around the chair and accidentally bumped into it. She slightly stumbled before Micah's strong arms caught her.

"This feels familiar," he voiced as he helped her to her feet without releasing his hold.

"Uh-huh…sure does," she replied breathlessly. *Don't look at his lips! Don't look at his lips!*

"Ready to go to your office?"

Crap! Man he has sexy lips! Soft and inviting... Why did he have to look at her like that? Like his main purpose was to always be her hero. *Say something!*

"Oh, um, yeah, okay, that works, um, let's." *What the heck did I just say! Great! Now I'm back to sounding like a blubbering idiot.* At the sound of a few giggles, Lex turned her head, having forgot that Imani, Cyd and Mya were still in the office and were witnessing the entire scene.

Way to go, Lex! How about you have a couple more embarrassing moments so that your friends will really have something to talk about.

As he followed Lex to her office, Micah couldn't hide the smile that crossed his face. Lex was frazzled, and he loved when she got nervous around him. She had the same affect on him, but he could hide it better than she could.

He'd heard enough of her conversation with her partners to know that Lex was having a hard time avoiding his advances. And he was sure that she disapproved of the extra paragraph in his contract that ensured they would be spending a lot of quality time together over the holiday season.

"How about we go to the café on the corner for brunch?" Micah asked when they arrived at her office. When she turned around to face him, she twisted her mouth and squinted her eyes.

"I thought your contract said you are really busy in the mornings and afternoons."

So she did read that part. "That's true, except today I had to run some errands so I'll be going into the office later this afternoon."

"How convenient," Lex said as she began tidying up her desk. Micah could only assume she was trying to look occupied while she contemplated her response. He didn't mind because it gave him the opportunity to observe her more than he had in Imani's office. She had no idea how attractive she was. On occasion, he'd overheard her say that she assumed he liked the model-type. Little did she know, he much preferred her five-four petite frame and nice round ass that he was sure would fit perfectly in the palm of his hands.

"Okay, let's do brunch," she replied, breaking his thoughts. She sat down to remove her ballerina shoes and put on her winter boots. She'd barely made eye contact with him since they arrived at her office. He smiled as he thought about the last time he was in her office.

When she stood, she went to grab her coffee mug, but accidentally spilled the remaining contents on a stack of papers.

"Oh, shoot," she shrieked, grabbing some tissue and

dabbing the papers. It took all of Micah's focus not to laugh. He didn't want to make her even more uncomfortable. *Her clumsiness is so cute.* Only then did she chance a glance in his direction. He couldn't read her expression at first, but he was glad when he heard her laugh. He laughed along with her.

"Being around you makes me *more* clumsy."

"Well, being around you makes me do a lot of things I don't normally do," he said. *Like be celibate for over three months.* If his brothers knew, there was no doubt in his mind that he would be the object of their jokes for days. He was Micah Madden after all... Bad boy turned good and lover of all things female. Unofficially voted in high school as the number one panty snatcher and the sexiest. *Celibate for over three months?* Definitely a new record for him.

"Let's go," she said as she grabbed her coat. They walked half a block to the café in a comfortable silence. Lex wore a slight smile, and he wondered what she was thinking.

"You have a nice smile," he said after they ordered a couple of sandwiches and drinks. He had her order first so he could pay for both meals. When she looked hesitant, he reminded her that he was the one who'd invited her to brunch. Luckily, she didn't argue with him and they retreated to an empty corner table in the café.

"Thanks," she said, meeting his eyes. "I like your smile, too."

A compliment? "Finally warming up to me, huh?"

"Don't push your luck," she said with a laugh. "I have to be nice now that I'm planning your parents' anniversary party."

Micah bit into his sandwich and observed her in between eating. "From what I hear, you're always nice. Cyd consistently calls you the nice one."

Lex nodded her head in agreement. "That's usually true…except…"

Micah searched her eyes. "Except when it comes to me, right?" he finished when she didn't continue. Lex gave him a soft smile and tilted her head to the side.

"How about we start over?" she asked.

"Meaning, you want me to forget about the incident at Bare Sophistication?"

Her cheeks flushed. "Yeah, that wasn't my most shining moment."

"I beg to differ," he said, trying to ignore the way she licked her lips after the last bite of her sandwich. "You were so adorable that day. At the lingerie shop and then the dinner party."

"Not really," she said as she went into her purse and put on an extra coat of lipstick.

"Maybelline and Covergirl must love you," he said, nodding to the tube in her hand. Her eyes grew big as she shoved the tube back in her purse.

"My mother is a lipstick fanatic and so was my grandmother. I guess you can say they passed their fascination with lipstick down to me."

"Well it looks great on you," he responded as his eyes dropped to her ruby lips. She had perfectly shaped lips… lips that craved to be devoured. She began fidgeting with the sheer pink scarf around her neck.

"So, what did you want to discuss today?" she asked.

"Well," Micah said, clasping his hands together, "I know you received the contract so I wanted to make sure you were okay with everything."

She tilted her head to the side before leaning slightly

forward. "To be honest, I wasn't too happy that your contract was already approved and signed off on."

She stopped talking, but it seemed she still had more to say. "Is that all?" Micah asked.

"No," Lex said letting out a deep breath. "Since I'm the lead planner for your parents' anniversary party, I would like you to go through me for everything you need in the future. No more going behind my back to my partners. Deal?"

"That's reasonable," Micah said. "But in my defense, I only went to them because you always avoid me."

"I'll work on that," she said with a smile. "I did have a question about the December winter festival in your hometown. What day did you want me to arrive for the festival?"

She is not gonna like my answer. "Um, here's the thing. My family plays an important part in the festival and my parents are on the town council, so I will be down there for eight days."

"Okay," she said before taking a sip of her water. "So do you want me to arrive on the first of the eight days or toward the end of the eight days?"

"I need you to be there for the *entire* stay."

"What!" Lex yelled as she braced both hands on the table. Micah looked around at the curious glances from people sitting nearby before he leaned in closer toward her.

"I was originally thinking I could plan their anniversary here in Chicago, but that wasn't really logical. It makes more sense for the party to take place in Arkansas."

"So exactly why would I need to be down there the entire time you're there? We plan long-distance parties all the time at Elite Events Incorporated. We have vendor contacts everywhere, including Arkansas. Venues, florists, DJs…you name it!"

"Cranberry Heights, Arkansas, is not your typical Arkansas town. In order to plan the type of anniversary party my parents will love, you have to get to know the town and the people who live there."

Lex scrunched her face in irritation. *So much for us getting along.*

"Where would I stay?" she asked.

"My parents' house is large so you can either stay there with them like I will, or at the town's B and B."

"What reason will you give your parents as to why I'm visiting."

I was hoping she'd ask that question. "I'll tell them we're dating and I wanted to show you the town."

"Absolutely not," Lex said raising her voice again. "You have got to be kidding me."

"Do you have a better idea?" Micah asked.

"Yes," she said, crossing her arms over her chest. "You could go to the winter festival by yourself and avoid having to lie to your parents altogether."

Micah glanced at her chest before meeting her eyes again. "No can do. And quite frankly, it's in the contract and you asked me not to go to your partners about this so I was assuming that meant you'd be accommodating."

"Is Arkansas country living or city living?" she asked.

"Both," he said with a laugh. "You have something against farm animals?"

Instead of responding, she stood up and began putting on her coat. *I guess we're leaving,* Micah thought, taking his cue from her and putting on his coat, as well.

"You don't have to walk me back to the office," Lex said when they reached the outside.

"Okay." They stood there in silence for a few moments before Micah spoke again. "So, will you come with me to Cranberry Heights for the entire stay?"

She dodged a couple of groups of people walking by. "I'll have to think about it." She continued looking at him straight on.

"I understand," Micah replied. "Let me know your decision at Imani and Daman's party this weekend," he continued before turning to walk in the direction opposite of her.

"Wait," Lex said, gently grabbing his arm. "You were invited to Imani and Daman's Friends-giving?"

"Is that what they are calling the party?"

"Yes. Since we all spend Thanksgiving with our families, Imani and Daman plan a Thanksgiving with their close friends."

"Well, yeah, that's the party. Daman invited me last week."

"Great," Lex huffed.

"Tell me how you really feel."

"Sorry," Lex responded quickly. "I'll let you know my answer then. See you later." With that, she put on her hat and began walking back to her office building.

"Have a good day," Micah yelled after her. She turned slightly and gave him a half smile.

She's gonna say yes. She really had no choice. Micah knew exactly what he was doing when he put that clause in his contract. He was sure visiting his hometown was the perfect way to take her out of her element and, hopefully, get her to see another side of him. She was used to these pretty boys, and Micah definitely wasn't that. He was rough around the edges and damn proud of it. He intrigued Lex. He could tell. But she wasn't all the way convinced yet.

"Watch out, Lex," he said aloud to himself. She was a challenge and if there was anything Micah loved as much as he loved women, it was a challenge.

Chapter 4

Micah stepped out of his car and jumped in place three times before making his way to the parking meter. Although he had on two layers of pants, a turtleneck, a hoodie and a scull cap, he was still cold. He loved running by the lake and refused to let the chilly Chicago weather stop the workout regimen he'd developed over the summer.

Apparently, he wasn't the only one refusing to let the thirty-five degree weather halt their workout routine. The parking lot was half full and even the threat of snow didn't stop a few people from bringing out their bikes.

Micah put in his headphones and scrolled to his workout playlist and then stuffed his phone in his armband. Stretching at a nearby bench, he glanced at the white frozen lake and started his five-mile run.

When Micah and his five brothers were growing up in Arkansas they used to watch reruns of *Good Times* and imagine how it would be to live in Chicago. Early last year when he quit his job of seven years and announced he was starting a business with Shawn, his brothers and mom had been supportive, but his dad not so much.

Micah didn't know what he had to do to get his father's approval. At family events, he pretended as if it didn't matter that all of his brothers had a good relationship with their dad. But, deep down, it hurt to know that his dad viewed him as the black sheep of the family. Micah visited his parents more than any of his brothers, but no matter what, his relationship with his dad remained non-existent. He hoped that planning the anniversary party would finally change the way his dad viewed him.

Micah nodded to a few runners passing by and moved out of the way of a couple bikers. His adrenaline was finally pumping and warming up his body. He cupped his hands together and blew into them before taking out his gloves that he'd forgotten were stuffed in the pocket of his hoodie. The view of the skyline was beautiful even in frigid temperatures.

Even though he left the Arkansas P.D. with no intention of ever returning to the force, he was still grateful that he'd had an opportunity to be a police officer. The P.D. forced him to change his ways and focus more on helping people make better choices. He'd run into a number of lost young men with no male role models around to help show them the difference between right and wrong.

His phone rang, breaking his thoughts. "Hey, Shawn," he said as he stopped by a nearby tree and continued to jog in place.

"Hey, man, I was hoping I caught up to you. Cyd just got off the phone with Lex. She told her that she wouldn't be going to Imani and Daman's Friends-giving tonight."

Micah scrunched his face. "Did she say why?"

"She said she needed some time to herself, but Cyd told me she thought it had something to do with you being there tonight, as well."

Micah knew that was the case, especially since Lex had yet to let him know if she would be attending the winter festival. "Cyd's right," Micah replied. "I know what it is. I'll call Lex and tell her it's safe for her to come to the party."

"Okay, good luck, man."

"Thanks." Micah hung up the phone and promptly dialed Lex's number. It went straight to voice mail. He tried twice more just in case it was a bad connection, but both times the call went to her voice mail again.

Micah called Shawn back. "She's not answering," he said when Shawn picked up. "It's going straight to voice mail, so I assume she turned off her phone."

Shawn laughed before telling Cyd that Lex had turned off her phone, and then informed Micah that he was putting him on speaker.

"Micah, what number are you calling?" Cyd asked. He rattled off the number to her.

"That's her work cell number. I'll give you her personal number so you can save it in your phone." Micah entered Lex's personal cell number in the notes section of his phone before thanking Cyd. He dialed the new number, and she answered on the third ring.

"Hello," she asked.

"Hey, Lex, it's Micah." The other line was silent for a few seconds.

"Oh, what's up?"

He laughed into the phone. "I was just trying to figure out why you cancelled on Imani and Daman tonight. If it was because you promised me an answer about the winter festival, then I'd like to take the pressure off you."

"What do you mean?" she asked softly.

"You don't have to give me an answer tonight."

"Then when would I need to give you an answer?"

"How about next week?" She was quiet for a moment, and Micah wondered if she was finished with their conversation.

"You must think very highly of yourself to assume that you're the reason I cancelled my plans tonight," she finally said.

"Well, isn't it?" Micah questioned.

"No," she answered. "I realized I had double-booked tonight and I've been super busy lately. So instead of choosing which party to go to, I decided to take a free night to myself. And for your information, I already know my answer to your request."

Micah smiled, hoping her answer was the only answer he wanted to hear. "And that is?"

She sighed into the phone. "Wipe that smile off your face, I can feel it through the phone." She let out a slight laugh. "I'll stay in Cranberry Heights for the duration of the festival."

Micah did a celebratory fist pump before responding. "I knew you'd make the right decision."

"Yeah, well you didn't give me much of a choice."

"Then I'll see you tonight? Everyone wants you there."

There was another pause before she responded. "See you tonight, Micah."

After he hung up the phone, he sent Shawn a quick text telling him that Lex would be attending the party tonight after all. A gust of wind made him shiver and he decided to cut his run short and head back to his car. Lex said that he wasn't the reason she had cancelled on the party, but he didn't believe her. It didn't matter either way because not only was she going to the party now, but she was also accompanying him to his hometown. And he planned on taking advantage of every moment he spent with her.

Lex lightly shook her wrist and watched the red wine swirl around inside her glass. She couldn't stare at her wine all night, but she could definitely plan to stare at it long enough to avoid Micah, who had invaded her space in Imani and Daman's kitchen. Their large estate with a gorgeous view of Lake Michigan had an enormous basement that Daman deemed the man cave and the entire six bedroom, five bathroom home had more than enough space to host their bimonthly get-togethers and holiday gatherings. But somehow, Micah had managed to pop up in the same room she was in three times tonight.

She didn't care that Cyd, Imani and Mya were in the kitchen, as well. Not only was the wine helping her hide her discomfort to his presence, but they were too consumed with talking about their newest clients at Elite Events to notice her lack of interest. She could feel her body heating in desire as he bent over in the fridge to grab a beer bottle.

Lord have mercy, she thought as she stole a couple glances in his direction. His loose-fitting blue jeans did nothing to hide the imprint of his butt, and his black-and-gray button-up seemed to only accentuate his muscular arms. And Lord knew she was infatuated with muscular arms. She'd never had the pleasure of dating a man who was as fit as Micah. Guaranteed, her ex, Evan, was in shape, but he definitely didn't have a body that looked that good.

He turned from the fridge quicker than Lex had anticipated and caught her staring. He shot her a half smile before popping off his beer cap and taking a quick swig. She took a sip of her wine as a distraction and was glad when a few people entered the kitchen to say their good-byes. She was relieved when Micah took that time to leave the kitchen, as well.

"I have a great idea," Cyd exclaimed, clasping her hands together. "Since most of the guests are leaving, how about we play a group game or something."

"Well the guys are downstairs playing cards," Imani said. "What type of group game did you have in mind?"

"A drinking game!" Cyd exclaimed.

"What are we, in college?" Mya chimed in.

Cyd cut her eyes at Mya. "What's wrong with a drinking game?"

"I agree with Mya," Lex added. "We're too old for drinking games."

"Well, I'm with Cyd," Imani said, getting up from the stool she'd been sitting on. "Let's play."

"Of course you both want to play a drinking game," Mya responded crossing her arms over chest. "With Daman and Shawn here, you can both get drunk and make love to them afterward. What are Lex and I suppose to do when we get all drunk and horny."

"Oh, come on," Cyd said as she shook Mya's arms loose. "Daman still has a couple single friends here and flirting never hurt anyone. Besides," she continued as she glanced over at Lex. "Don't you want to see Lex try to ignore her attraction to Micah?"

They cannot be serious. "Um, I'm not playing," Lex said.

"It won't be fun without you," Imani said as she leaned in to hug Lex.

"You mean, it won't be fun if you don't have me to laugh at."

"What if we promise not to laugh?" Cyd asked. *Oh, brother.* They weren't going to let her back out of the group game easily.

"I'm only playing the game if Mya agrees to play, too." All eyes turned expectedly on Mya.

"I'll play," she said with ease as she shrugged her shoulders. Lex squinted her eyes at Mya in frustration.

"Great! I'll go get the guys so we can gather in the grand living room!"

"I'll come with you," Cyd said as she followed Imani out of the kitchen.

Lex flared her hands once Imani and Cyd were gone. "Um, Mya? What happened to the two of us sticking together?"

"A girl can't change her mind?"

Lex blew out a frustrated breath. "Not when there's so much at stake!"

"Okay, maybe I missed something. What exactly is at stake by us playing this game?"

Lex thrust her head to the ceiling and closed her eyes. If she admitted that she didn't trust herself around Micah when alcohol was involved, that would mean she would have to admit that her self-control was low around him. She wasn't even ready to admit that to herself so she definitely wasn't going to admit that to Mya.

"Whatever," she said brushing it off. "Let's just go get this game over with."

As they rounded the corner and walked the hall that led to the grand living room, Lex's heart was beating so fast, she swore she could actually hear the sound of it echoing through the hall. She felt as if she were walking into the lion's den, with Micah being the lion and her, his prey. *You got this, girl. It's just a game and he's just a man.* But the minute she entered the room, she knew she was in trouble. His piercing brown eyes landed on her, breaking the little cool she had.

Cyd had already directed everyone in a circle and the cards on the large coffee table were spread sporadically in a circle, as well.

"What is this game?" Lex asked as Cyd, she and Mya took a seat next to one another in the circle, as Cyd had instructed to with her index finger. They'd played group games before, but this wasn't their usual Q&A game and it definitely involved more liquor than usual.

"It's called circle of death or ring of fire. Whatever name you like most. I personally like circle of death so that's what we're calling it tonight."

Say what? Circle of death? Who in their right mind would play a game called circle of death? Lex finally noticed the beer can in the middle of the table. Shot glasses and mixed drinks were also in front of everyone. She lifted up one of the red cups and inhaled. *Tequila? Oh, heck no. I'm not drinking this!*

"Um, Cyd?" Lex asked, holding up the red cup. "What's in this cup?"

Cyd gave her a sly smile before responding. "That's tequila my dear, but don't worry, I watered yours down with juice. And before you tell me you refuse to drink it, how about I explain the rules of the game? Because if you pick your cards right, you may not have to drink that much."

Lex flashed Cyd a fake smile before she put the cup down.

"You'll be fine," Mya whispered in Lex's ear before glancing across the room. "I got your back."

She followed the line of Mya's eyes and landed right on the same person she'd been trying to avoid the entire night.

"Yeah, right," Lex whispered back. Lex could handle her liquor and usually loved a good game. But having Micah in the room made her nervous, and her friends knew that tequila was her kryptonite. Therefore, she avoided the stuff like the plague.

"Lex you pick a card first," Cyd prompted. *Please be a good card. Please be a good card. Yes, a three! Wait, what's a three?*

"I have a three," Lex said to the group. "What does that mean?"

"A three stands for *me*," Cyd said. "Which means you have to take a drink."

Of course that's what it means. Lex reached for the red cup.

"Not that one," Cyd said. "Your first drink has to be a shot."

"Fine," Lex said through gritted teeth. She swung back the shot and placed the glass back on the table with more force than necessary.

"Mya, you're next."

Mya picked a four, which meant that all the women had to drink. "I hate this game already," Lex said in what she thought was a whisper. She glanced at Mya,

Cyd and Imani in time to see them all trying to stifle a laugh. When she glanced across the table at Micah, he seemed to be holding back a laugh, as well. Lex loved a good laugh just as much as the next person, but lately, it seemed that all jokes were on her.

Chapter 5

Since it was the group's first time playing this particular game, Cyd had stated they would only go a couple rounds. Micah thought it was nice to revert back to their college years when drinking games were a thing of the norm, but most people in attendance were in their upper twenties and thirties, so their tolerances weren't nearly as high now as they were back in college.

Micah could tell that Lex was trying her best to keep her composure because, apparently, liquor made her a lot bolder. She wasn't shy about batting her eyelashes in his direction, and on a couple occasions he saw Mya hold Lex's hands down to her sides. Each time, he wondered what Lex was about to do that caused Mya to grip her hands.

"It's you turn, bro," Shawn said breaking his thoughts. He'd surprisingly pulled a number that hadn't been pulled yet.

"Cyd, what's a five?" She glanced over at Shawn and gave him a slick smile before she answered Micah's question.

"Well, like I said, there are many different versions to this game. But for tonight, a five means that we have to play *never have I ever.* Let's just do a rotation around the circle and each person says something that they have never done before. For kicks, let's put up five fingers, too. If you have done it, we trust that you'll be honest and put down a finger if you have. If you run out of fingers, participate anyway for fun."

Seems simple enough. "Okay," Micah said as he tried to think of a good *never have I ever* confession. "Never have I ever been fired from a job," he said deciding to keep it general. He may have quit his fair share of jobs when he was younger, but never had he been fired from one. A couple of Daman's friends and one of Imani's friends put one finger down.

"Never have I ever hot wired a car," Daman said next, receiving a few groans from a couple men, Micah included.

Imani was next. "Never have I ever been arrested." Micah was hesitant to put down a finger with Lex watching him so closely, but he promised to be honest.

"Didn't you used to be a cop?" Lex blurted out. *Damn, I knew she was looking.*

"Yes" was all Micah said. If she wanted to know the story, she'd have to wait.

"My turn," Cyd said. "Never have I ever skinny dipped," she continued as she gave Shawn a hard stare.

"Baby, I told you I didn't like how that lake looked," Shawn said firmly. "Besides, you're forgetting about the whirlpool in Carbondale last year."

"Making love to me in a hotel whirlpool is not skinny dipping," Cyd said poking her finger at Shawn's chest.

"What about all those times in Anguilla?"

Cyd blushed and lowered her voice. "Oh, yeah, all those times in the ocean…swimming pool…natural spring pool."

"TMI guys," Mya said shaking her head with a laugh. "We can still hear you and that sounds like a conversation for the bedroom."

Shawn and Mya took turns next, and then it was finally time for Lex's turn. *She's beautiful,* he thought as he watched her contemplate what she wanted to say. She had gotten up from her chair and was now sitting on the floor with her legs crossed. The color of her skinny jeans and blouse made him think about the lilac lingerie set he'd seen her purchase a few months ago. Damn, what he'd give to see her in that. Her hair was pulled up in a high ponytail and once again, she was wearing lipstick, only today, it was a color he hadn't seen before. She caught his eyes before she spoke.

"Never have I ever done anything in my life that was spontaneous or against the rules." Micah took note of the sad look in her eyes as she glanced around the room and saw finger after finger drop from people who had done what she confessed she hadn't.

When the next person went, his eyes still remained on Lex. She was playing with the rim of her cup, but her mind looked as if it were miles away. Before he could think about what he was doing he interrupted the game.

"Sorry everyone, but I think I need some fresh air," he announced. "Lex, would you like to join me on the patio outside?"

She gave him an incredulous look. "It's like twenty degrees out there."

"I'll get our coats."

She still looked skeptical, but luckily, the women talked her into joining him. He hadn't been outside yet, but he'd heard Daman talking about the rectangular bonfire table and outdoor furniture they had on the patio.

"It's freezing," Lex said as soon as they stepped outside into the darkness.

"Let's sit over there." He pointed to the chairs stationed around the bonfire. He sat on the bench and she took a seat two chairs away from him. He observed her as she blew into her hands before rubbing them together to stimulate friction. Even with the wine and tequila, she still didn't look completely relaxed.

"Why don't you sit here by me so I can warm you up?" She turned up an eyebrow at him. "I just meant we would stay warmer if we were sitting closer together. More body heat," he continued. She didn't need any more convincing as she began to move to sit beside him.

"So," she said, slightly turning to face him, "what were you arrested for?"

Man, she wasted no time asking me that. "How about I tell you that story when you're a little more sober."

"I'm sober now."

"Not completely."

"Nothing's wrong with my listening skills."

He searched her face. "I think I'll wait."

She looked disappointed. "Can you at least give me a hint?"

Micah laughed as he shook his head. "You already know that I used to be a cop, so clearly I'm not a bad person."

"I never said you were a bad person, but you do seem like a bit of a troublemaker," she said, brushing away a few strands of hair that had escaped from her ponytail.

"How can you tell?" he asked. "You've barely given yourself a chance to get to know me."

"Oh, I can tell," she said with a laugh. "You get this sneaky look in your eyes right before you're about to do something or say something to rattle someone's nerves." *So she has been paying attention.*

"That's not enough to label me as a troublemaker."

"Hmm…okay. From what I've observed over the past few months, I can tell that you're arrogant, cocky and a womanizer."

"Whoa," he said as he placed his hands over his chest. "Arrogant and cocky…at times, yes. Why? Because I'm a confident person. But a womanizer? That's far from the truth."

She gave him a look of disbelief. "You're a class A flirt, Micah, and I'm sure you'd screw anything with a skirt and not even care about how she felt afterward."

Ouch. That hurt. Especially coming from Lex. "Okay, yeah, I like to flirt. And I love being surrounded by beautiful women. But what man doesn't?" Micah got closer to Lex to make sure that she was listening to every word. "But I'm selective in who I date and who I sleep with. A womanizer is a selfish, egotistical prick that manipulates women and cares too much about himself. Whereas, I like to cherish women. I value their opinion, and although I've chased a few skirts in my time, now I'd much more prefer to date just one woman."

Her eyes grew bigger, and he noticed a quickening in her breathing. She didn't say anything and slightly turned her head away from him, so he continued.

"You see, Lex, for months I've been trying to get to know you but, apparently, you have already convinced yourself that I'm no good for you. Now, I'll admit that every now and then I can cause a bit of trouble, but I promise," he said as he lightly touched her chin to bring her face back toward him, "my kind of trouble is pleasurable and satisfying."

He watched a range of emotions cross her face, the most prominent emotion being interest. He'd seen that look on her before, but tonight was different. Tonight he'd learned that Lex was the type of woman who followed the rules. She thought before she took action and if something was out of her comfort zone, she backed away from it. Micah knew he was definitely standing outside of her comfort zone blocked by a gigantic electric wall. But he wanted to blow her fuse and he was pretty sure now was his chance to push her a little further.

He leaned in closer to her and to his surprise she began leaning forward, as well. When they were mere centimeters apart, she hesitated and slightly parted her lips, releasing a small fog only visible in the frosty breeze. *Keep going, Lex.* He wished he could grab her and finally get the kiss he'd been waiting on for months. But he needed her to make the decision to move just a tad closer first. Her breaths grew quicker, letting out faster puffs into the cold air that matched his own and mingled into one white cloud between them.

"Remember what you said during the drinking game?" Micah asked, noticing a cute small brown freckle on her nose that he hadn't seen before.

"During never have I ever?" she asked breathlessly.

"Yes," he said. "Don't think, just do." She searched his eyes before dropping to his lips. She leaned in a couple more centimeters. *That's close enough,* Micah thought as he crashed his lips to hers. He expected her to be surprised, but instead, her hands went around his neck as she softly moaned into his mouth. She tasted just like he'd imagined she would…sweet and tangy with a hint of wine and tequila from the game they'd been playing.

He probed her mouth open even farther and slipped his tongue deeper inside when she parted her lips more. She moaned softly into his mouth and gripped his neck even tighter, lightly massaging the back of his head as she did. The seductive way she moved her hands just made him want to kiss her harder…longer…until they were both breathless and craving for oxygen. What was it about this woman that pushed him to the brink of insanity? He'd never been this intrigued by a woman before, nor had he enjoyed a kiss quite like this. When she moaned into his mouth again and slipped her tongue even deeper, he knew he had to stop before he lost complete control of himself.

He broke the kiss, heaving rapidly as his lungs filled with coldness. Her cheeks were pink and her lipstick smeared. Evidence of just how thoroughly he'd devoured her mouth. "That was some kiss," he voiced, saying the first thing that came to mind. In all honesty, he didn't know what to say because all he wanted to do was to continue kissing her.

Her eyes grew from seductive to big and cautious. *Oh, no…what is she thinking.* Before he could even ask her what was wrong, she hopped up from the seat, said she had to go and hightailed it back into the estate.

Micah wanted to go after her and knew whoever was still at the party would take one look at her flustered state and swollen lips and be able to tell she'd just gotten thoroughly kissed. But he couldn't move from his spot on the bench. He looked down at the bulge of his pants and tried to will it to go down. But it was useless. There was only one person who could make it go down and, unfortunately, she'd run from him once again.

"Way to go, Madden," he said to himself as he unbuttoned his coat and hoped that the harsh wind would help him calm down.

As soon as Lex stepped back inside Imani and Daman's estate, she went straight toward an empty bedroom that was a couple feet away from the door with a window that overlooked the patio. She kept the lights off when she entered and softly shut the door behind her. Taking a deep breath, she pushed back the curtain to see if Micah was still sitting by the bonfire.

He was right were she'd left him and by the look on his face, he was just as affected by the kiss as she was. She had never been kissed like that, and even with the cold temperature, her body felt like it was on fire. She brought her hand to her lips, a little surprised by their swollen state. He put every man she'd kissed in her past to shame, and if that kiss was any indication of how good he was in the bedroom, she was in trouble.

While she watched him stare at the bonfire, she wished she knew what he was thinking. There was something so rugged and mysterious about his demeanor, and even though she wished she wasn't curious about him…she was. She wondered what led him to become the man he was today. And what had he been arrested for? He ran one hand down his face and smiled. *To be inside his mind,* she thought, wondering what his smile was about. She hoped he was smiling because he was thinking about her. His response to her accusation about him being a womanizer had left her speechless. Not only had she offended him, but she'd also made assumptions based off little fact. He probably thought she'd kissed him because she was a little intoxicated, but she'd only pretended to drink the last couple times she was prompted to during the game, so she was alert. She'd kissed him because at that moment, she wanted to know exactly what his lips felt like…tasted like. For months, she'd convinced herself that kissing him wasn't what she wanted to do, but in that moment, she decided to do something she didn't do often. React before thinking about the consequences.

He pushed his coat off a little more and dropped his head back. He'd unbuttoned his coat despite the fact that the weather outside was slowly growing even colder. He placed both hands over his face and sat like that for a couple minutes. When he adjusted himself on the seat, she couldn't see his face, so she opened the curtain a little more, moving closer to the window to get a better angle.

He placed his elbows on his knees before standing. His face looked strained for a moment, until he shook out his arms and rolled his neck. When he stretched his arms in the air, his back was turned to Lex. She watched him completely remove his coat and throw it on the bench before shaking out his arms for a second time. *It's freezing! Why in the world is he removing his coat?*

Her question was answered the minute he turned around and she noticed the massive bulge in his pants. She gasped and brought her hand to her mouth, wondering how she'd missed it when she was outside with him. He looked down at his pants before looking up to the sky. Watching him standing outside, completely aroused just from sharing one passionate kiss with her was enough to wet her center to the core. She placed one leg in front of the other, clasping her thighs together as tightly as she could.

I wish I had the nerve to invite him back to my place. She quickly shook her head at the thought. "Where did that come from?" she asked herself quietly. He began pacing back and forth, the bulge in his pants slowly diminishing. She quietly giggled to herself when she finally realized that the only reason he was still outside was because he was trying to calm himself down before heading back into the estate.

He jumped in place a couple times before grabbing his coat and turning toward the window Lex was standing at. "Oh, crap," she said before dropping the curtain. The lights were off so there was no way he could see her. *But he looked right in my direction, so maybe he did see me standing here.*

She quietly made her way to the door just as she heard the back door leading to the patio slide open. When she saw the knob turn, she quickly jumped behind the bed.

"Lex, are you in here?" Micah whispered into the bedroom. When she didn't respond, he said her name again. *This is stupid,* she thought when she imagined how crazy it was for a grown woman to be hiding behind the bed. She slowly rose, and was happy to find him still in the doorway looking into the dark room, unaware that she had been hiding.

"I'm here," she said softly as she reached the door. He pushed the door slightly open, leaving it cracked so that the light from the hallway could seep in.

"So you were watching me outside," he said as more of a statement than a question.

"Only because I wanted to make sure you were okay since you didn't follow me back inside."

"Did you enjoy watching me when you thought I hadn't noticed?"

She knew what he was doing. He was trying to make her feel uncomfortable, but she didn't want to give him the satisfaction. *Just be honest.* "Yes, I did enjoy watching you," she said confidently. His face was half hidden by the darkness, but she didn't miss the grin that crossed his lips right before he bent down to kiss her again.

You should stop him, she thought as her arms took on a mind of their own and curled around his neck. *He's your client and if you don't stop him now, he'll think he can kiss you whenever he wants.* His hands went around her waist and pulled her closer to him. Once again, his mouth explored hers, lighter than before, but still just as demanding. She was just about to push him away when she heard him let out a deep groan as one hand sprawled across her back, while the other gently cupped her butt. She could feel him getting excited all over again, and the fact that he didn't care that she could feel the length of him excited her way more than she wanted it to. *Okay, maybe you can enjoy this last kiss before you tell him it could never happen again.*

And that's exactly what she did.

Chapter 6

Lex looked at her cell phone for the fourth time in the past thirty minutes. Usually, it only took her about ten minutes to get her eyebrows done, but the place she normally went to closed early on Fridays. She'd taken one look at herself in the mirror and knew she had to tame those bad boys before she met Micah for dinner.

She glanced around at the women in the waiting area to make sure no one was watching and slowly eased the back of her feet out of her heels. She was furious with herself for wearing heels to impress a man today of all days. It had been raining nonstop and not only were her feet wet and her shoes squishy, but her hair had decided to do a half straight, half curly look on its own. She'd spent all last night straightening her hair and this morning, she'd feathered it as well to add bounce and depth. Years ago, she'd grown out her relaxer and promised to never look back. Although she loved that her hair was healthier than it had ever been, Chicago was a hard city to maintain non-chemically-treated hair. Whether she straightened it or wore it natural, it sometimes decided to do exactly what she wished it wouldn't do.

"Mam, we're ready for you," the salon assistant said to Lex. *Thank goodness!* She hadn't seen Micah in a week and since they were leaving for Arkansas in a few days, she had to set some ground rules that she knew he wouldn't like. After the intoxicating kisses they'd shared a week ago, it would be hard to ignore his advances but she had to. She would be there to do a job…nothing more. And the quicker Micah realized that, the easier it would be to convince herself that he was no good for her.

"All done," the eyebrow specialist said to her after she was done threading her eyebrows. Lex settled the payment and tip and left the salon.

Goodness, she mouthed as she noticed several people on the corner trying to hail a taxi. The bus stop was a couple blocks away, and the new umbrella she'd just bought was clearly for fashion and not rain. She wouldn't have a weapon against the rainfall.

She decided to walk across the street from the other taxi hopefuls, and luckily she was able to get a taxi right away. When she arrived at the sushi restaurant that Micah had chosen for dinner, she was just on time for their reservation.

"Hello, Micah," she said, taking a seat at the table he was already at.

"Hi, Lex," he replied, watching her every move as she removed her coat. She had chosen to wear a black skirt that hugged her curves in all the right places and a blue blouse with a few ruffles in the center that offered a peak of her cleavage. She completed her outfit with modest silver jewelry and sleek black pumps. All her partners in the office earlier had mentioned how great she looked, but more importantly, she felt great.

"You look amazing," he said to her after she'd sat down. The appreciation in his eyes momentarily stole her breath and made her forget about her aching feet.

"Thanks…you look great, too," she responded, taking note of his sharp black suit and name-brand loafers. She hadn't seen him in a suit in a while and, apparently, seeing him all dressed up still had the same affect on her. She crossed her legs under the table and tried not to look too closely at his lips, which was a challenge as neither one of them said anything. In the comfortable silence, all they could do was observe one another. Instead of looking at his lips, she looked at his hair, noticing for the first time that it looked different than she remembered.

"Trying something new with your hair?" she asked. His curls were a little fuller at the top and the sides were cropped short in a fade that made his devastatingly sexy look even more masculine.

"Just changing it up a bit," he said, shrugging his shoulders and flashing her a smile.

"It looks nice." *So nice that I wish I could run my fingers through it.* Before her mind could wander any more, the waiter came to take their order. Lex had more than a few questions about the daily special and the top-rated dishes at the recently opened sushi restaurant. After a few minutes of back and forth discussion with the waiter, she finally placed her order and turned back to Micah as he placed his order, as well.

"So I take it you really love sushi?" Micah asked.

"I'm a huge fan of sushi, but I like all types of food."

"What's your favorite dessert?" he asked.

"That's easy! Anything red velvet!" *Who didn't love mouthwatering chocolate,* she thought. *I bet he's even tastier than chocolate.* She shook her head, reminding herself that comparing Micah to anything that was mouthwatering would surely make her drool in public.

"I actually love red velvet cake myself. What's your favorite type of food?"

She took a sip of her water and smiled before responding. "Honestly, I love food too much to pick just one type. Indian. Italian. Greek. Soul food…I could go on forever."

"I see," he said with a laugh. *Just great, Lex…way to sound like your favorite pastime is eating.* Which it was, but she didn't need him to know that.

"Based off the questions you asked the waiter, I can tell you have a great food palate."

Good, he seems more interested than turned off. "My dad is a huge foodie and a great cook so I guess you can say I got my love for food from him."

"Do you love to cook like your dad, as well?"

"Definitely," she answered just as the waiter placed their plates on the table. "When I was little, I would watch him in the kitchen all the time so naturally, as an adult, I mirrored a few of his techniques and turned them into my own."

"Hmm, techniques. So you're a whiz in the kitchen, huh?" he asked as he popped a piece of sushi into his mouth.

"I throw down every now and then," she said, nodding her head. She took out her phone and snapped a quick pic of the sushi before uploading it to her Instagram account and hash-tagging the restaurant.

"Sorry," she said when he was looking at her curiously. "I'm a bit of an Instagram fanatic and I love tagging things from new restaurants and events."

She slid her phone over so he could see a few of the images. "Most of these are foods I cooked myself."

"Nice pics," he said after he'd scrolled through several. "Any chance you'd ever let me taste some of your cooking?"

Everyone knew how much Lex loved cooking, but she hadn't cooked for a man in years. "We'll see," she said, taking her first bite of food and glancing at him as she chewed. He was charming and she hadn't really seen this particular side of him before, not that she'd given him much of a chance. He hadn't said anything about the kiss and if she hadn't known how much he enjoyed it at Imani and Daman's party, she would have questioned if the feelings were one-sided.

Conversation between them flowed easily as they talked about a few more things related to food, cooking and random shows on the Food Network.

"So you're a fan of *Top Chef?*" she asked, surprised.

"Sure am," he said, flashing his pearly whites. "Although I probably can't cook as good as you, I like to watch *Top Chef* and a few other shows on the Food Network to brush up on my skills."

My, oh, my. I love a man that can cook! If there was any weakness that Lex had besides a man with a nice butt and muscular arms, it was a man with good teeth and a love for cooking.

"I'll cook for you, if you cook for me," she blurted out without thinking.

"Just name the place and time sweetheart." His astute smile was unmistakable and his statement triggered something inside her. *Sweetheart?* He hadn't called her that before and the fact that she'd gone about eight years of her life being called sweetheart by a man she'd rather forget existed was unsettling. This wasn't how the conversation was supposed to be going. She liked how easy it was for her to talk to him, but she hadn't addressed any of the issues she had planned to discuss at tonight's dinner.

He steered you away from your plan, the voice inside her head taunted. Lex lived off plans. That was how she made sure her life ran in order, leaving little room for mistakes. But Micah was a mistake that she wished she could convince herself to make. Not only was he not in her life plan...he stood for everything she convinced herself she didn't need. This was exactly how her ex had trapped her. Charming her and calling her pet names. His favorite was sweetheart. As a matter of fact, the only name he called her was sweetheart. *Ugh!* Micah could have called her anything but that, and she'd still be captivated by him and the conversation.

"Micah, there's something we need to discuss," she said ignoring the confused look on his face.

"Are you okay Lex?"

"Yes," she said directly. "I forgot to tell you at the party that although I agreed to go with you to the winter festival, we will have to refrain from kissing and behave professionally."

"Um, okay," Micah said, looking at her with concerned eyes. "But my parents think they're meeting a woman I'm dating. Won't it be weird if we don't kiss."

"Everyone won't expect PDA."

"Knowing how I am...they will."

She wished his statement didn't warm her body. "Well, if we have to share a kiss or two for show, that's fine. But nothing more. And I will stay at your parents' home because if they are anything like my family, they won't allow me to stay at the inn when we are supposed to be dating. But we must have separate rooms."

"That can be arranged," he said, searching her face. "Did I say anything to offend you?"

She sighed as she contemplated the right words "No, you didn't say anything," she lied, finishing the remainder of her food. He seemed as if he wanted to ask her more, but her phone rang, halting their conversation.

"Sorry, I need to take this call," she said to Micah as she rose from her seat and went to the waiting area of the restaurant.

"Hi, Mom."

"Oh, Lex, so glad I got you! Is there any way you can stop by the house tonight?"

Lex glanced at her iPhone to check the time. "It's almost 8 p.m. If I take the train, I still won't get out to the suburbs until about 9:30. Can this wait until tomorrow?"

"Oh, okay. I understand," Linda Turner said into the phone in disappointment. "Your father and I are driving to Tennessee with your aunt and uncle, Hope and David, and we leave at 4 a.m. tomorrow. But it's okay, I guess it can wait until later. I just really wanted to see you before we left."

Lex recognized the tone in her mother's voice and knew it was definitely not okay. Her mom was more than just a mother. She was one of her greatest confidants and Lex hated to hear her disappointed.

"Okay, Mom, I'll stop by. But I won't be able to stay long."

"No, you're right, sweetie. I don't want you traveling home this late. I'll just see you when you get back from Arkansas."

She'd told her mom the entire story and the way Micah conned her into going to Arkansas with him. To her dismay, her mom thought the entire situation was hilarious.

"Excuse me, Lex," she heard Micah say behind her.

"Hold on, Mom," she said before placing her hand over the phone and turning her attention to Micah.

"Yes."

"The waiter brought the check so I went ahead and paid and grabbed your coat and purse since this place is getting pretty packed with the late dinner crowd. Would you like to go across the street for coffee so we can talk about the Arkansas trip?"

More time with you would be too tempting, she thought. And though they still had more to discuss, she now had other plans.

"Sorry," she said to him. "I have other plans tonight." She saw the hint of disappointment in his eyes and tried not to enjoy it too much. For the past ten minutes she'd been acting pretty firm toward him and although she knew he didn't understand her change in demeanor, she couldn't help it.

"Okay, do you have any time tomorrow?"

She tilted her head and looked into his eyes. She didn't have any plans tomorrow except a bit of winter cleaning, but he didn't have to know that. *I wonder if I should make him think I have a hot date?* She was normally honest with men, not caring one way or another if they knew the truth. But Micah rattled her nerves too much and she was slowly realizing she enjoyed toying with him when she could.

Don't do it Lex, her inner voice warned. "Sorry, but my plans tonight may be *exhausting*," she said, ignoring the warning and emphasizing the word *exhausting*. "My companion may keep me up too late." As she watched the displeasure spread across his face, she secretly relished in the fact that he wasn't ready for their night to end.

He didn't say anything. Instead he just stood there watching her closely. When she felt her nerves roll into a ball at the pit of her stomach, she pushed the feeling away. She felt liberated…in control. Powerful. Feminine. Strong.

"We'll just catch up when our schedules match, Micah," she continued.

"Baby, you better stop lying to that man." Her mother's voice filled the front of the restaurant. The high-pitched voice caught her off guard and caused her to almost drop her phone. She glanced down and realized she'd accidentally hit the speakerphone key. *Stupid touch phone.* She tried to click the speakerphone off, but it wasn't working.

"That man just asked you a simple question and you are making up excuses not to spend time with him. If he's as sexy as you say he is, then you should take him up on his offer for coffee."

"Mom, you're on speaker," Lex yelled into the phone. "I'm trying to get you off, but I can't," she said nervously, tapping the phone.

"Am I still on speaker?" her mom asked.

"Yes," Lex answered, not daring to look up at Micah.

"Oh, good. Put the phone near Micah."

"He can still hear you mom."

"Micah?" her mom called out.

"Yes, Mrs. Turner?" Lex finally glanced at him, mortified to see him grinning from ear to ear.

"Is there any chance you can drive my daughter to my house right now? Her father and I have something important to give her."

You have got to be kidding me. "Mom, he can't do that."

"Of course I can, Mrs. Turner. We're leaving the restaurant now."

"Micah, this isn't necessary."

"Oh, yes it is," her mom responded. "Lex, let Micah bring you over here. And your father and I want to meet him."

"Mom, we'll be there," Lex said, accepting defeat. "See you soon," she continued, prompting her mom to disconnect the call.

As soon as her mom hung up, her phone conveniently unfroze. All she could do was shake her head and look down at the floor. Without looking into his face, she grabbed her coat and put it on before taking her purse. *So humiliating.* Stuff like this would only happen to her.

Chapter 7

Once they were outside, she looked up at him again, happy to see that he was no longer smiling. The sunlight was gone, but the streetlights and snow on the ground still illuminated the area. Micah pointed his hand to the left for her to walk in that direction.

"How far down did you park?" she asked.

"Three blocks," he answered, falling into step with her. When they had walked two blocks, she couldn't take the silence anymore.

"Don't you have anything to say?" she asked him.

"Nope, nothing," he stated frankly. *Oh, I get it. He's paying me back for lying to him about having a date.*

Why did men make things so complicated? Micah always threw her off, yet she says one little white lie and he gets all bent out of shape.

She looked at him again. His face hadn't changed.

"Okay, fine," she said tossing her hands in the air. "I'm sorry for lying to you."

"I can't believe you lied," he said as he turned to her with a solemn look on his face. "My ex used to lie to me all the time."

He placed his head down and grew silent again. *Just great, Lex. Lie to the guy who has a history of women lying to him.*

"Well I truly am sorry, Micah. I was just trying to get you back for all those times you made me feel uncomfortable."

"Because you think I'm such a bad person." His voice was desolate, and Lex felt even worse. She reached out to touch his hunched-over shoulders. When she did, he caught her wrist and brought her to him. She gasped out of surprise.

"What are you doing?" she asked Micah, attempting to push against his chest but instead, she rested her hands there. He flashed her a mischievous smile.

"You're not upset at all, are you?" she asked him, finally catching on.

He laughed before he responded. "What type of sensitive men have you dated in the past that would cause you to believe I was upset about something so small."

Evan would have been furious. "I thought I'd hurt you're feelings," she said, feeling gullible that she'd fallen for his antics once again.

"Hurt my feelings?" he said, looking into her eyes. "Words don't break me. Besides…you think I'm sexy."

"My mom said that, not me."

"I've never met your mom, so I can only assume that she was quoting what you've told her."

He was leaning in closer to her and she knew what he

was about to do, yet she wasn't trying to stop him. In fact, she wanted it just as much as he did. When he was close enough to almost touch her lips, an ambulance flew by, disrupting the moment. It was the chance Lex needed to push away from him.

"Are we near your car?" she asked, walking ahead of him.

"It's a couple cars down," he said, following behind her. When they reached his car, he opened the passenger door so that she could slide in.

When he was walking around to the driver's side, she let out the breath she'd been holding. Her night wasn't really going the way she'd planned.

"Just so you know," she said, turning to Micah when he got in the car, "I meant what I said earlier. No more kissing."

He shook his head and laughed as he started up the engine.

"I mean it," she said, trying to sound forceful.

"I heard you when you said it in the restaurant," he said, turning his attention to the road. When they stopped at a light, he looked over to her, determined and resolute. "But if you think I'm forgetting about those explosive kisses we shared, then think again. You'll see."

See? What would she see? She wasn't sure she could handle seeing anything more Micah had to offer, which she was sure was a helleva lot.

"What's the address?" he asked, breaking her thoughts. She rattled off the address so he could plug it into the GPS system in his car.

"Let's go meet moms and pops," he said with a slick smile. She didn't dare respond to his comment. Words had gotten her in enough trouble tonight. Instead, she turned to look out her window and prayed that news of her introducing Micah to her parents wouldn't spread in her family like wildfire. Having one set of parents believe they were a couple was enough drama for one holiday season.

After a thirty-minute drive, they arrived at her parents' house. She had no idea what her parents wanted to give her, but she knew it had to be important if they wanted her to come visit them this late. When they pulled into the driveway, her parents were already opening the front door.

"Hey, baby," her dad said, embracing her as she stepped inside the house. She hugged her mom and her dad before introducing them to Micah.

"Mom, dad, this is Micah Madden. Micah, these are my parents, Linda and Ethan Turner."

"Nice to meet you both," Micah said, hugging Mrs. Turner and shaking hands with Mr. Turner. Lex smiled as her dad sized up Micah. Since she was an only child, her dad was extremely protective, especially after her relationship with Evan.

"Why don't we go sit in the family room," her mom stated after they removed their coats and shoes. When they sat down, she observed each parent, wondering why they seemed so anxious.

"Would you like me to wait in another room?" Micah asked, clearly sensing their apprehension, as well.

"No, that's not necessary," Mrs. Turner stated.

"What's going on?" Lex asked.

'Well, sweetie," Linda said, slightly glancing from her to her dad, "your father and I were able to locate something and were so excited to give it to you that it couldn't wait until Christmas." Her mom pulled out a white box with a blue bow tied around it that had been sitting on the table near the large sofa.

"Open it," her mom said, handing her the box. She looked at her parents inquisitively before untying the ribbon and opening the box.

When she removed the tissue paper, her heart skipped a beat. She let out a soft gasp as she clenched her chest, overwhelmed by what she saw. *It can't be...* She picked up the delicate gold brooch and ran her hands across the gems and diamonds. She hadn't seen the brooch in years and thought she'd never see it again.

"How did you find it?" she asked her parents.

"Your father was with some friends in Michigan and he ran across the brooch in an upscale pawnshop."

"What," Lex exclaimed. "Michigan! He sold my brooches to a pawnshop in Michigan!"

"Sweetie, that doesn't matter," her mom responded. "What matters is that your father was able to find it or better yet, the brooch was able to find him."

Lex knew her father often checked pawnshops to see what hidden treasures were waiting to be found. It was truly a miracle that he had found this one. "This must have cost you a fortune," she said to her dad.

"Nothing's too expensive for my baby," her dad said as he gave her a wink. Lex walked over to where her parents were sitting and gave them each a huge hug as she thanked them while rubbing away a couple tears that had fallen.

"Did you find the others?" she asked, although she already knew the answer. If they had, they would have given them to her.

"No, I didn't," her dad responded, sounding crushed.

"Well then, I'll make sure I cherish this one." When

she returned to her seat, she met Micah's curious glance before dropping her eyes back to the brooch. She heard her mom tell her father to join her in the kitchen before they vacated the room.

Once she was alone with Micah, she figured now was a good time to mention a part of her past that she often tried to forget.

"This brooch is one of three," she said, turning her head to face him. "When I went off to college, my grandmother Faith Gamine Burrstone, my mom's mother, had given me one of three brooches that were given to her by a dear friend. She knew I always loved them, and when I was little I used to sneak into her room, put on her lipstick and fancy wigs and stick one of her brooches on my shirt as I pretended to be her. I couldn't get enough of playing dress up with Gamine's stuff," Lex said with a slight laugh.

"Every time she caught me, she just smiled, gave me a kiss on the cheek and told me that one day, she would give me a brooch when I was old enough to hear the story behind them. I was surprised and honored when at eighteen, she had decided to give me a brooch from her collection…but there hadn't been a story to go along with it. She said that there would be a story she'd tell me later when I was ready to hear it."

Lex momentarily glanced back at the brooch as emotion clogged her throat. "When she passed away six years ago, she left me the other two brooches in her will along with the story that I'd waited most of my life to hear. It changed me at the time of her death, and it was exactly what I needed to hear in my life at that moment."

She glanced back at Micah, a little surprised at herself for what she was about to share with him. It was a topic, she rarely spoke about…mainly because she had a hard time admitting to herself that the woman too cautious for her own good had been reckless in her past decisions.

"The day I received the story and the other brooches was the day I decided to divorce my ex-husband, Evan Gilmore." She stared into his eyes, waiting for the look of shock or surprise to cross his face, but it didn't.

"Did someone tell you I was divorced before?"

"Not at all," he said as he took her hands in his. "And I'm sure divorcing your ex wasn't easy."

"It wasn't," she responded, glancing at their intertwined hands before looking up to his face. "On top of being the worst husband in the world, he also robbed me of my youth, among other things. A week before I was moving out of our home, we were robbed and the thieves managed to take everything I cherished in life… including all three of my grandmother's brooches. I always suspected Evan was behind the robbery, and so did my family. My suspicions were confirmed a year after our divorce when one of Evan's old coworkers told me that he had overheard Evan at the gym the day before the robbery gloating to a couple other men that if I got half of what he had earned, then it was only fair that he take the things I loved, as well. So my dad finding this brooch is priceless…"

"I'm sorry to hear that," Micah said with concern written across his face. "What did he do that made him the worst husband?"

She opened her mouth to say more, but then closed it quickly. *How can I possibly explain the depth of the hurt he caused?*

"You can tell me when you're ready," he said, sensing her hesitation. "But I do have one thing to say."

I don't want your pity, she thought. He reached up to touch her cheek. "The hardships and pain that we must go through sometimes may feel unbearable. But it's those situations and circumstances that make us stronger and wiser. It may not feel like it sometimes, but your relationship with your ex made you stronger...not weaker."

His words melted her heart in a way that no one else had. So many of her friends and family knew about her relationship with her ex, yet Micah had managed to listen to part of her story without judgment or pity. The man looking at her with his rich brown eyes was not flirting or joking like he normally did. He was compassionate, and although she knew she shouldn't kiss him, that was all his words made her want to do.

She leaned closer to him, enjoying the glint in his eyes when he, too, realized that she was going to kiss him. She never took the initiative to kiss a man, especially a man like Micah. Her lips softly brushed his at the same time that her hands clasped the back of his neck. He quickly took over, dipping his tongue into her mouth. She sighed from the sweetness of his lips. The kiss wasn't too hard or too soft... It was perfect with just the right amount of pressure. She could go on kissing him forever, which was exactly why she needed to end it before they lost control.

When their lips broke apart, she didn't feel the same anxiety she felt around Micah the last time they'd kissed. This time, she felt comforted, calm, and...protected. Those were feelings she hadn't felt from a man in a very long time.

Chapter 8

Micah stood in the kitchen listening to Mr. Turner explain the best way to smoke a turkey. It was the fourth dish that he'd pulled out of the refrigerator since he and Lex had arrived. When Lex had told her father that Micah enjoyed cooking, it hadn't taken him long to have him taste a range of dishes he'd previously made.

"Now taste this macaroni and tell me if you can pinpoint my secret ingredient," Mr. Turner said, handing Micah a small plate. Micah tasted a bite of the macaroni and turned toward the kitchen entrance, wondering where Lex and her mom had run off to.

"So…what do you think?" Mr. Turner prompted. Micah turned his head back to Mr. Turner at the sound of his voice.

"Hmm…did you add a little cayenne pepper?" he asked.

"Exactly," Mr. Turner said, snapping his fingers. "Plus a special cheese that you can only import from Italy." *Lex wasn't lying about her father's love for cooking,* Micah thought as he laughed to himself. He'd learned more cooking secrets from Mr. Turner in the past hour than he had on several Food Network shows.

Mr. Turner's checkered glasses and animated expressions reminded Micah of his uncle Barry, who used to wear unique glasses and spoke with such emotion when he was passionate about something. They would have gotten along wonderfully and since they were both talkers, he couldn't imagine them running out of things to say. Too bad his uncle Barry was no longer here and his own uptight father wasn't blessed with the gift of gab.

His mind drifted back to Lex. He knew it had been hard for Lex to tell him she had been divorced, but little did she know, it explained a whole lot about her character. Now Micah understood why Lex seemed so dismissive of him at times. Her ex had put her through a terrible marriage followed by a hellish divorce, and then taken things from her that she held dearly.

"Micah, are you ready to go?" Lex asked as she entered the kitchen wearing a smile that he couldn't seem to get enough of. Her mom trailed closely behind her. It was obvious that Lex had gotten her natural beauty from her mother, although she favored both of her parents a great deal.

"I'm ready," he said before turning back to Mr. Turner. "It was nice to meet you, sir, and I enjoyed our conversation."

"It was nice to meet you, too," Mr. Turner said shaking his hand. "Make sure you take care of my daughter in Arkansas."

"I will." After bidding goodbye to Mrs. Turner, Micah escorted Lex to the car. They plugged her address into the GPS and began the drive to her home. Glancing over at Lex, he smiled when he noticed the content look on her face. He didn't know if it was the brooch or their conversation that made her seem more at ease. But he figured it was probably a combination of both. At every stoplight on their drive to the expressway, he couldn't help but glance over at her.

"Any reason you keep staring at me," she asked, turning from the window to look at him, trying to hide the smile on her face.

"No reason," he said, looking from the road to her. He thought she would question him some more but she didn't. She leaned her head against the seat and her eyes fluttered closed, another good sign that she was getting more comfortable around him.

Halfway through their drive, Lex's breathing was even and peaceful as she slept. She wore a slight smile on her face that made him wonder if she was dreaming about the kiss they'd shared. He hadn't planned on kissing her in her parents' home, but when she had leaned toward him, he couldn't help but capture her lips.

His personal cell phone rang and he briefly wondered if he should let the car pick up the call or answer on his Bluetooth. He chose his Bluetooth so he wouldn't disturb Lex.

"Talk to me."

"Hey, Micah. It's Shawn."

"What's up, man?"

"I just heard from the Wellington brothers. We got their investment, but there are still a few minor things we have to do before they sign the contract. I already asked our lawyer to go over the termination clause and other details."

"That's great news. I'm meeting with Grant and Parker Inc. in Little Rock, Arkansas, next week. I think we're pretty solid and can count on their investment, but of course I'll update you after the meeting."

"Sounds like a plan. Landing that account would be our biggest yet. Good luck in Arkansas."

"Thanks, man," Micah said before hanging up and glancing at Lex to make sure he hadn't disturbed her sleep. He had been looking forward to their trip to Arkansas ever since Lex had agreed, but after tonight, he was even more anxious to see what the coming weeks would bring.

"Excuse me, Driver. How much longer before we get to Cranberry Heights?" Lex asked after seeing nothing but open fields for the past half hour.

"The welcome sign for Cranberry Heights is right up the road, mam," the driver replied. "Then it's about ten minutes until we get to the Madden manor."

Just as the driver had stated, the welcome sign came into view. She stared out the window and admired a cluster of horses running in a meadow. She honestly couldn't remember the last time she'd seen so much outland. She had expected to be traveling with Micah to Arkansas, but last minute, she'd changed her flight and told him she would meet him a day after he arrived, claiming she had some last-minute work to finish. But in actuality, she had been overanalyzing what type of clothes to pack and gathering everything she would need for a two-week trip. Not to mention, most of her brain had been occupied with thoughts of Micah's sweet kisses, wondering what it would feel like to have his mouth in other places.

A large banging noise distracted her from her thoughts. "They must be setting up for the winter festival, right?" she asked the driver.

"Most of the festival is already set up, but they are preparing for the kick-off parade tomorrow morning. All of Cranberry Heights comes out for that festival as well as a few neighboring towns."

"Interesting," Lex stated as she observed the men and women decorating the parade floats. She cracked her window to let a little air into the heated vehicle. The fifty-five degree Arkansas weather was a big relief from the eighteen degrees she'd left in Chicago, but the Arkansas residents appeared to be as bundled as Chicagoans. The town seemed quaint and festive. Lex's family was big into the holidays, but she had a feeling she was in for a surprise here in Cranberry Heights. Already, she'd seen signs advertising a variety of winter activities.

As they passed through the part of town that she assumed was downtown, and turned on a long coiling road with houses in the distance, her mind became occupied with thoughts of Micah again. Her parents had enjoyed meeting Micah and although they'd promised not to mention their visit to other family members, she knew better. *If I weren't so attracted to him, I probably wouldn't even care...* But the fact that she was so attracted to him was exactly why she did care. Guaranteed she was a little clumsy by nature, but around Micah she oftentimes felt more awkward than usual, and instead of coming off as sexy, she came off as a klutz. *Maybe I should just head back to Chicago?* she thought when she remembered that

Micah's parents would be under the assumption that she was dating their son.

"Mam, we're here," the taxi driver said to Lex as they pulled up in front of Madden Manor. She rubbed her hands together, a sign that she was anxious, as she stared at the massive house, not yet ready to get out of the vehicle. The large white house was gorgeously decorated with an array of Christmas decorations. She could only imagine how amazing the house looked at night. Pine trees surrounded the right and left side of the home, and a rustic welcome sign was displayed on the front door. Lex was in awe of the entire decor and probably would have sat in the car gazing at the house even longer if the driver hadn't tapped the window.

"Sorry! I was admiring the decorations," she said as she finally got out of the vehicle. "How much do I owe you?"

"Mr. Madden already took care of it," the driver replied as he began wheeling her bags up the gravel sidewalk.

"At least let me give you a tip," she said after him, pushing the fifty-dollar bill back in her wallet and reaching for ten dollars instead.

"No need, mam," the driver said with a smile when they reached the front porch. "Mr. Madden already took care of that, too. Enjoy your stay."

After the driver left, she turned toward the front door and was just about to ring the doorbell when the door flew open.

"You must be Lexus," said an older woman with soft brown hair, creamy mocha skin and kind eyes. Her facial features were warm and inviting and, immediately, Lex felt comfortable.

"I'm Cynthia Madden, Micah's mother. My son has told us so much about you. Come in out that cold dear."

"Nice to meet you, Mrs. Madden," Lex said when she stepped inside the foyer.

"Now, do you prefer Lexus or Lex? Micah mentioned both names to us."

At least he had the decency not to mention LG or lingerie girl as one of my nicknames. "Lex is fine," she replied, unbuttoning her winter coat. "You're home is so beautiful."

"Thank you," Cynthia replied as she took and hung up Lex's coat. "My husband doesn't always appreciate my interior decorating skills, but I always tell him that it's important for our guests to feel as if they are in their home away from home."

"I agree," Lex replied, following Cynthia into the living room. "What smells so delicious?"

"That would be my apple crumb pie," Cynthia said with a smile as she led Lex to the living room. "How about I bring you a slice and a cup of coffee before I give you a tour?"

"That would be great," Lex replied, her mouth already watering.

"Then, I'll be right back. Please make yourself comfortable. Micah is getting firewood from the shed so he should be back shortly."

After Cynthia left, Lex took the time to admire the decorations inside the home. The large pine tree was decked out in silver-and-gold ornaments while green vines wrapped around the staircase. Antique Christmas angels were delicately placed throughout the few rooms in the house that she could see from where she stood in the living room, and white lights outlined the top of the ceiling in every room.

The soft Christmas music playing in the background reminded her of her grandmother's home during the holidays. Her grandfather still made sure the house was decorated for the holidays, but her grandmother Gamine had an extra special touch that the family had missed since she'd passed away.

Lex breathed in the earthy scent of pine and cedar as she walked over to the massive fireplace to admire the red velvet stockings hanging there and on the near wall. There had to be about twenty stockings in total. *Why on earth are there so many?* Her eyes grew bigger when she zoomed in on a stocking with the name Lexus written on it.

"That's so sweet," Lex said to herself.

"My mom is the sweetest person I know," Micah said behind her before he placed an armful of wood in the black wrought iron log rack. *Don't watch him bend over,* she reminded herself when she felt her eyes following his movements. She focused on a quilt placed over the side of the couch for distraction, admiring the unique patches and warm colors. *Thank goodness we have separate rooms.* Just being in the same vicinity as Micah now was hard enough. She couldn't imagine how it would be if they had to spend the night in the same room.

"I'm glad to see you have arrived safely," Micah said, coming to stand close to her. She turned to face him and immediately wished she'd focused on a spot behind him instead of on him directly. His striking stance demanded her undivided attention.

"You look good," Micah said as his eyes traveled the length of her. Before she'd left for the airport this morning, she'd chosen to wear a pair of skinny jeans, a white blouse and brown boots. She didn't want to seem as if she was trying hard to impress him, but in actuality, it had taken her almost an hour to pick out her outfit.

"You look good, too," she said observing his loose-fitting jeans and beige button-up. "We complement each other."

"I agree," he said, his eyes dancing with laughter. "We look good together."

Wait, I didn't mean it like that. "I meant our outfits complement each other."

"That, too," Micah replied as he glanced at her lips. He took a step toward her and she wondered what he was going to do.

"Don't worry," he said as he reached out his arms to pull her closer to him. "I was just going to hug you," he whispered in her ear. The mellow tone of his voice made her skin tingle with desire. She was slowly learning that everything Micah did was for a purpose. So the calculated way he pulled her into his embrace and the way his lips brushed against her ear were both things that he'd done on purpose…perhaps, just to rattle her.

"Yeah, I'm sure that was the only thing on your mind," Lex responded with a slight laugh after he released her. He flashed her a smile showing off his deep dimples. *Goodness he's sexy.* She really loved the curly Mohawk style he wore and he had a sort of rugged look about him today that added to his sex appeal.

"Well, I have to tell you, Lex," Cynthia said, returning with a piece of pie and coffee, "I don't think I've ever seen my son smile that way at a woman. You must be someone special."

Lex glanced at Micah to see how he would respond and was intrigued to see that he was still smiling.

"Mrs. Madden, I noticed the stocking with my name on it," Lex interjected, changing the subject. "Thanks so much for including me even though I won't be here for Christmas."

"Didn't Micah tell you?" Cynthia asked as she placed a cup of coffee and slice of pie on a nearby coffee table.

"Tell me what?" Lex asked, looking from Micah to his mother.

Cynthia gave Micah an incredulous look before explaining. "Next week, we are having an early Christmas celebration with our guests who are residing in the B and B this month."

"Oh, I didn't know that," Lex responded, picking up the pie to take a bite. *That would explain all the stockings.* "Sounds fun! I'm looking forward to that. And this pie is wonderful, Mrs. Madden."

"Thank you, dear," Mrs. Madden said with a smile.

"Is the B and B nearby?" Lex asked, taking a sip of the coffee.

Cynthia glanced at her son again. "Madden Manor is also a B and B. It's actually the only one in town. We currently have all of our rooms occupied except the room that you and Micah will be sharing together."

Chapter 9

Sharing together? Lex thought, almost choking on her coffee and spitting it all over the living room. Oh, heck no, she must have heard her wrong. "Micah and I are sharing a room?" Lex asked after she quickly placed the coffee back on the table and cleared her throat.

"Of course you two are. My husband and I weren't born yesterday. You're both adults and we're filled to capacity because of the festival."

"Well, um, right. Adults. That's us," Lex said with a nervous laugh. "We are adults. That we are. Two adults who are dating and sharing a room together. That's normal." She sounded confused even to her own ears. And she couldn't stop laughing or talking in between laughs.

"Yes, it is," Mrs. Madden said as she drew her eyes together in concern. "Are you okay, dear? You seem a little nervous about something."

"Me? Nervous? Not at all. Never nervous. Not me." *Pull yourself together Lex! And please stop this awkward laugh lingo!* Lex told herself as she cast her eyes to the ceiling. *You sound like a crazy lady.*

"I just can't wait to see how big this manor is," Lex exclaimed, waving her hands for implication and spinning around in a circle. When she stopped her 360-degree spin, she was finally able to keep her mouth closed. She knew her face looked flushed and her cheeks were puffed out in annoyance, but she couldn't help it. Micah had guaranteed her that they would have separate rooms, and she wasn't prepared for Mrs. Madden's news.

"Are you sure you're okay, cupcake," Micah said, stepping in front of Lex and rubbing his hands up and down her arms. "You do seem nervous, but you have nothing to be nervous about. I'll take great care of you while you're here." He then lowered his voice and glanced over to his mom and explained that she was nervous about country living. *Cupcake? Country living?* She could deal with the pet names and staying in Cranberry Heights, but playing house with Micah every night was *not* in her plans.

Lex put on her best award-winning smile and willed her hands to stay by her side, and not react on instinct and push Micah away. Micah's back was now to his mom so Cynthia couldn't see the spec of challenge in his eyes that dared Lex to declare their relationship as false. Well, she had news for him. Now that she had committed to this charade, she was going to put the couple of late-night theater classes she'd taken in college to good use.

"I know you'll take good care of me love muffin," Lex exclaimed pinching Micah's right cheek. When he smiled even harder, she pinched his cheek harder.

"Ouch," Micah finally said, pushing her hand away

and releasing his hold on her. "Save your spunkiness for later, baby," he said with a wink.

Oh, I can't stand him. "Mrs. Madden, how about that tour?"

Cynthia looked inquisitively from Lex to Micah before clasping her hands together. "Okay, then. Why don't you sit down and finish your pie and coffee. I'm going to wash a few dishes, then we can start the tour."

"I'll help you, Mom," Micah said, not giving Lex time to question him without his mother present.

Two things came to mind as Lex stole a glance at Micah and his mom when they walked out of the living room. One, she never had a choice where she was staying since her only options had been Micah's parents' place and the town's B and B, which turned out to be the same place. Two, she barely trusted herself around Micah when they weren't residing in the same living quarters. She had absolutely no idea how she could control her hormones with him sleeping right beside her in bed.

She's so nervous, she can barely concentrate on the tour, Micah thought as they made their way from the library to the east wing of the manor where several of the bedrooms were.

Madden Manor was one of the first homes built in Cranberry Heights so it had a lot of history. When his parents had moved there when he was in high school, he hadn't appreciated the home or the town. Now that he was older, he valued both a great deal.

"Here is the bedroom you both will be staying in," his mother stated as they arrived at the end of the hallway. Micah was glad that they'd gotten the most secluded guest bedroom in the house. It was also one of three bedrooms with a connecting bathroom.

"It's beautiful," Lex stated as she browsed around the room, her eyes briefly stopping on the massive wooden canopy bed before moving to the French antique furniture.

"It smells amazing in here," she stated as she glanced at his mother.

"That's my special ginger and cinnamon holiday blend in the oil burner on the nightstand. There is a burner in every bedroom. I started creating special oils when my husband and I decided to turn our home into a B and B. There used to be another B and B in town, but it burned down a few years ago and the owner decided not to rebuild it. The only option guests have is to reside here or a neighboring town."

"I love it. I remember you saying you are full to capacity. Where is everyone?" Lex asked.

"My father took the guests on a historical tour of Cranberry Heights," Micah answered. "Most of the guests arrived a couple days ago for the festival."

Just as Micah had responded to Lex's question, they heard the sound of chatter and commotion coming from downstairs.

"That must be them now," his mother said as she began making her way to the door. "Micah brought your bags up here when I was washing dishes. I'll let you both freshen up before dinner, then I'll introduce you to everyone."

"Okay, and thanks so much for your hospitality," Lex said. Micah's mother gave a soft smile before she exited the room. He cracked the door and took a seat on the burgundy chair in the corner of the room as he watched Lex walk to her belongings and open up her suitcase.

"Do you mind if I take the drawers on the left side of the bed?" she asked. Micah shook his head and laughed. *She's barely glanced my way since we stepped into this bedroom.*

"I don't mind. I took the drawers on the right already anyway."

"Okay, that works," she said as she began taking out jeans, tops and socks. He liked the way she curled her nose as she took out every outfit, and he wondered what she was thinking about. Suddenly she stopped unpacking and glanced over her shoulder at him. "Are you just going to sit there and stare at me while I unpack my clothes?"

"I was thinking about it," Micah said as he crossed his arms behind his head and leaned back in the chair. She turned to completely face him with disapproval written all over her face. *You've really pissed her off now, Madden.*

"You've got a lot of nerve, Micah," she said as she began walking toward him. "First, you add this obscene clause in your contract with Elite Events forcing me to accompany you on your hometown visit. Then, you ask me to agree to this imprudent plan of yours to allow your parents to assume we're dating. And as if things couldn't get any worse, we have to sleep in the same room when you promised me my own space."

When she stopped her rant, she looked at him as if she wanted him to explain why he'd done those things. But truthfully, he didn't have much to say. "Everything you said is true," Micah stated as he rose from the chair and went to stand in front of her. "I added that clause in the contract and I knew it was unorthodox. I came up with a plan that I knew my parents would eat up. And I promised you a separate living space while you're here, and now we will be breathing the same air every night."

Lex's eyes enlarged before she spoke again. "And..." she said, rotating her hands to imply that she was waiting for him to say more.

"And what?" he asked with a shrug of the shoulders.

"What about an apology?" she asked, placing her hands on her hips.

"LG, I'm not apologizing," Micah said with a laugh.

"Don't call me that," she said through gritted teeth.

"But you'll always be lingerie girl to me," he said, stepping closer to her. She may have worn an annoyed look on her face, but the air around them was charged with awareness. "Unless you'd rather I call you runaway girl."

She squinted her eyes together and tilted her head to the side. "Why would you call me runaway girl?"

Did she really have to ask? "Maybe because every time we get too close, you get scared and run away. It's what you do."

Her face displayed a mixture of interest and embarrassment. "You don't know me," Lex said, stepping closer to him. "Like now," she said, removing her hands from her hips and crossing her arms over her chest instead. "I'm not running now...am I?"

Micah wasn't one to stand off with a woman, but if he really thought about it, usually the women he dated ran after him...not away from him. She looked like she wanted to back down, but she stood there.

"Are you daring me to give you a reason to run to prove something to me?" Micah asked, dropping his eyes to her lips. "Or are you trying to prove to yourself that you can handle being around me without running."

She licked her lips and uncrossed her arms, returning her hands to her hips. "Want me to be honest?" she asked.

"Always," he answered.

"A little bit of both," Lex said quietly. "I'm cautious in my approach to a lot of things and when I'm uncomfortable, I run." The look in her eyes made Micah think back to the drinking game they'd played at Imani and Daman's estate. He didn't know if he was taking the moment out of context, but he felt as if Lex was giving him permission to push her to her limit. Whether that limit be with him or otherwise, he was ready to accept the challenge.

"I have a proposition for you," Micah said, ignoring her wary look.

"In addition to the propositions you've been giving me since we met?"

"This is different," he said, collecting his words. "While you're here in Arkansas, I want you to indulge in something with me."

She raised an eyebrow at his statement. "Meaning?"

"I want you to try and do or say something that's out of your comfort zone each day. And at least one has to be something you do without thinking about the consequences."

Her features softened and he could see the wheels in her head turning. He wanted to add that taking a chance on him would be something spontaneous and out of her character, but he didn't want to push her. She was thinking too hard already, but he didn't mind it at the moment. It gave him the opportunity to observe her more closely than he had earlier. She had no idea how sexy she was. It wasn't an over-the-top sexy or a blatant sexy. Lex had more of a natural sex appeal that surfaced when she wasn't even trying.

She sighed and shuffled from one foot to the other. *I wonder if she realizes that she's still staring at me.* Her mind seemed miles away so he figured she didn't notice. Otherwise, based on his past experience with her, she would have turned away so that her thoughts weren't so visible to him.

He had a remedy for all her thinking. Every part of him was drawn to her so he could only imagine how good it would be when they finally made love. She had to accept that fact in her mind first, but that was a big reason why he wanted her to come to Arkansas. He was hoping a change of scenery would put her in a different state of mind. Although many would call him a city boy now, he still had country roots. He only knew city-girl Lex, and now he was hoping to see another side of her.

"Okay, Micah," she said, breaking his thoughts. "I accept your proposition to live a little more spontaneously while I'm here in Arkansas."

A slow smile crept on his face the instant he heard her agree to his proposal. "You won't be sorry," he said, not caring if she picked up on his excitement.

Micah wasn't sure what Lex was about to say before there was a knock on the door.

"You can push it open," he said to the person on the other side of the door. When his father came into view, Micah's smiled slightly faltered.

"Hello, son," his dad said walking into the room. "And you must be Ms. Turner." His dad reached out to shake Lex's hand. "I'm Mason Madden, Micah's dad. It's nice to finally meet you."

"It's nice to meet you, too, Mr. Madden," Lex said, returning his handshake. "And please call me Lex."

"Very well," his dad responded before turning his attention to Micah. "Your mother wanted me to let you know dinner will be served in ten minutes."

Micah and his dad hadn't talked much since he'd arrived so he knew his father was making an effort since Lex had arrived. "Thanks, Dad," Micah stated. It didn't matter how old Micah got, he couldn't ignore the look of disapproval on his father's face. His father looked as if he was going to say more, but decided against it.

"Very well," his dad said as he left the room. Now it was Micah's turn to busy himself and avoid any questions.

"Did you and your dad get into an argument?" Lex asked. *Yeah,* Micah thought with a strained laugh. *About twelve years ago and he still has yet to forgive me.*

"Not recently," he answered instead. Lex's inquisitive eyes were evidence that she had a lot more questions to ask.

"Can I ask you something else?"

Not if it's about my dad. "Sure, what's up," he said as he stepped into the bathroom to wash his hands. She followed behind him and let out a sigh of amazement.

"It's gorgeous," she said running her fingers over the granite countertop before she made her way to the waterfall shower and separate whirlpool tub. "I can't believe this is the room your parents let us stay in."

"I can," he said, grabbing a paper towel to dry his hands. "I've never invited a girlfriend to stay with me at Madden Manor before so I knew my mom would go all out to make you feel at home."

Lex gave him a soft smile before examining him again. "About my other question," she said, standing closer to him. "Do you and your dad have a close relationship?"

"That's a loaded question," Micah said, leaving the

bathroom and making his way to the door. "The short answer is, it's complicated. But it's time for dinner so let's discuss this another time."

He didn't give her a chance to respond and walked out of the bedroom. He was aware he was being slightly rude, but talking about his relationship with his dad would have left a negative tone in the bedroom and that was definitely the last feeling he wanted to have lingering in the air.

Chapter 10

"We're here folks," Mason Madden said to the small bus of Cranberry Heights visitors. When Micah's parents had informed the guests that they would arrive two hours before the kick-off parade to secure their seats, Lex had felt right at home. Oftentimes in Chicago, one had to arrive early to all public events to secure a good spot. It seemed the same was true for the town of Cranberry.

The sidewalks and streets were already filled with residents and visitors excited for the parade to start. Holiday music was playing on speakers located on every street corner and happy families were dancing and singing along. Lex had been to plenty of parades in her lifetime, but there was something mesmerizing about the sight she was seeing today.

"Let's set up here," Cynthia Madden said to the group as she pointed to one of the few open spaces left. Lex opened the lawn chair that the Maddens had given each of the guests and continued to observe her surroundings. There were four couples and two families residing in the B and B, and Lex had enjoyed all of their company at dinner. She sighed when she thought about Micah last night. At dinner, he'd done his best to keep up appearances and appear unaffected by whatever had happened between him and his father in the bedroom, but Lex could read between the lines.

While the other guests had eagerly dived into Mrs. Madden's scrumptious apple crumb pie, Micah had informed her that he had to take care of a few things before the parade. She'd planned on staying up and waiting for him to return to the room, but she'd fallen asleep and hadn't awaken until the next morning only to find his side of the bed empty. She should have been thrilled that she'd avoided the first awkward night with him, but instead, she felt as if something was missing since she hadn't seen him since yesterday evening.

"Mind if I keep you company," Cynthia asked, breaking Lex's thoughts. "Micah is still helping a few of the parade participants set up."

"I don't mind one bit," Lex replied as she helped Cynthia open her chair. She had only known Micah's mom for a day, but she felt like she'd known her for years. When Cynthia looked over her shoulder and gave her husband a soft smile, it made Lex think about the upcoming anniversary party she was planning, and she figured now was a great time to ask Mrs. Madden some personal questions.

"You and Mr. Madden seem so close. Is it too personal if I ask how you and your husband met?"

"Of course it's not too personal," Mrs. Madden said as

she draped a blanket across her and Lex. "I met Mason about thirty-six years ago when I was in New Jersey, the state I grew up in. I had gone into a restaurant with my boyfriend at the time and I'd noticed Mason instantly. Mason had been dining with some friends of his, but by the look of interest on his face, I could tell he noticed me, too. That day is memorable to me for a couple reasons. That was the day I was proposed to twice. And it was also the day I met the man of my dreams."

"How did you receive two proposals?" Lex asked, completely engrossed in the story. Cynthia smiled before continuing.

"My boyfriend at the time proposed to me at the restaurant. I knew he would propose soon, but what I didn't expect was the knot in the pit of my stomach coercing me to say no. I said yes, ignoring my body's warning and convinced myself I'd made the right decision. As soon as my date excused himself to go to the bathroom, Mason walked over to my table and told me congratulations before he leaned down to whisper in my ear..."

"What did he say?" Lex inquired when Mrs. Madden appeared to be lost in thought. Cynthia placed her hand gently over her heart and tilted her head to the side.

"He told me that I should not have accepted the marriage proposal. And when I politely asked him why, he said, with confidence and vigor, that he was the man I was supposed to marry and that if I left with him that day, he was positive we'd be married that time the next year."

"Oh, my goodness," Lex exclaimed as she propped one leg up in her chair and did a ninety degree turn to face Cynthia. "How did you respond?"

"I slapped him in the face," Cynthia said with a laugh. "I couldn't believe he had the audacity to even approach me after I'd just accepted a marriage proposal. But then, something strange happened that made me rethink my decision."

"What was that?"

"While I was berating him for being so rude, he bent down and captured my lips in the most seductive kiss I'd ever had. A kiss that was seen by all the patrons at the restaurant, including my fiancé of ten short minutes."

"I can't believe Mr. Madden did that."

"Neither could half the people in the restaurant." Cynthia continued to smile as she finished the story. "The restaurant manager actually escorted my fiancé back to the table and asked Mason to leave the restaurant. Of course, being the stubborn man he is, Mason refused to leave without me." The look of contentment that Cynthia had on her face whenever she stole glances at her husband melted Lex's heart.

"Mason was always a bit of a bad boy and he was never one for following rules. At least that's how he was when we were younger. Having children made him more responsible and forced us to both grow up."

"What did you do when they kicked Mason out of the restaurant?"

"I did what I thought was right and followed my heart," Cynthia said looking straight into Lex's eyes. "I told the manager and my fiancé that if Mason had to leave, then I was leaving with him, and I handed my fiancé back the ring. Surprisingly, although the manager, my ten-minute fiancé and I were shocked, the person who seemed the most surprised by my choice was Mason. As soon as we stepped outside the restaurant, he asked me why I'd chosen him when I didn't know anything about him. At first, I wasn't sure how to answer. But the more I looked into his handsome face, the more my heart melted. So I told him the only thing I could…the truth."

"What was the truth?" Lex asked, hanging on Cynthia's every word.

"The truth is something that still remains true today," Cynthia continued. "I told him that the kiss we shared made me feel more alive than anything I'd ever experienced, and I wasn't ready to let that feeling go. Right then and there, Mason kissed me again with more emotion than he had in the restaurant. The kiss was so amazing, it left us both breathless and at a loss for words."

Love at first site in the truest form. Lex had heard stories of people who fell in love instantly, but this story seemed like a scene plucked right out of a classic romance movie.

"Neither of us had realized that we had an audience, or that Mason's friends were witnessing the scene with wide eyes of disbelief. I remember the ring that Mason was wearing on his pinkie finger that day. In front of all those people, some strangers and some not, he asked for my hand and placed the ring on my finger. He didn't propose marriage, but he did propose a promise that if I moved to Little Rock, Arkansas, with him and allowed him to court me, he'd make sure our marriage was always filled with love and devotion."

"You've got to be kidding me," Lex exclaimed as her hands flew to her mouth. "Obviously, you eventually moved to Arkansas, but what did you say to his proposal?"

Cynthia looked at Lex and laughed. "I said yes and met him in Little Rock two weeks later. Six months later we were married and ten months after we were married we had Malik, my oldest son."

"From New Jersey to Arkansas! That's so brave of you," Lex said in disbelief. "I went through a really bitter divorce over six years ago. Knowing what I know now, I can't imagine changing my entire lifestyle for a man."

Cynthia reached over and gently squeezed her hand. Lex wasn't sure why she'd shared that information when she rarely acknowledged that she'd been married before, but she felt compelled to share it with Micah's mom. "I can tell two things by your statement," Cynthia said. "First, your ex-husband was not the man you were sup-posed to be with because God had other plans for you. And second, my son hasn't given you a proper kiss yet that will make you so weak in the knees that you can barely speak."

Lex wasn't certain how her face looked, but she was pretty sure a deer caught in headlights was accurate.

"When a man truly kisses the woman he knows he wants to spend the rest of his life with, that kiss will touch the depths of her soul and build a permanent home right on top of her heart. A lot of people thought my re-lationship with Mason was just lust or a case of bad-boy syndrome as my friend used to call it. But Mason and I knew differently. After the type of kiss that we shared, we owed it to ourselves to try and have a relationship. We celebrate our 35th anniversary soon, so as you can see, I have no complaints and six beautiful sons to show for it."

"Six sons!" Lex repeated loudly before she could stop herself. Cynthia gave her a puzzled look. *If you were dating one of her sons, of course you'd already know how many siblings he has.* She knew he had brothers, but not five of them. "I mean…I can't imagine not hav-ing a daughter. It must have been hard raising all boys."

"It sure was," Cynthia said with a laugh. "Boys and

girls are totally different breeds. I felt like I was pregnant for a few years straight. I'm sure Micah has told you how tall all his brothers are. Imagine making the newspaper every time you have a son with the headline being, Local Resident Breaks New Record With Largest Baby In Arkansas."

"I can't even imagine that," Lex said, making a note to ask Micah about the names of his siblings while she was in town. The only brother she knew about was Malik, who had attended Imani and Daman's wedding. "When did you and Mr. Madden move to Cranberry Heights?"

"Two of my favorite ladies," Micah exclaimed, not giving Cynthia a chance to answer. He bent down to kiss his mom on the cheek before turning toward Lex and planting a soft kiss on her lips. Usually, she'd be caught off guard by the kiss, but after talking to Micah's mom, the kiss felt natural. He lingered above her mouth for a while, both of them soaking in the sight of each other. He smelled masculine and woodsy, a combination that aroused every part of her body despite the cold air.

"Having a good time," he asked, his eyes remaining locked to hers.

"I'm having a great time." *Even better now that you're here.* She wished it weren't true, but it was. *I wonder if I'll ever have a love story to share in the future?* Evan definitely wasn't her fairy-tale story, but he took the cake for worst nightmare ever.

"You'll have that moment soon," Cynthia said, glancing between her son and Lex. *Huh? Did I ask that out loud?*

"What moment?" Micah asked, finally stepping back from Lex. *Okay, good. It was in my head.* But, by the way Mrs. Madden assessed her meant she'd probably keep an eye on Lex to see how she reacted to Micah while she was in Arkansas. Her best option was to fake her attraction to him when they were around his mom so that she couldn't read the truth in her eyes, but would still assume they were dating. *How can I fake attraction when I'm already attracted to him?*

"Micah, dear, how about you sit next to Lex and I'll go sit next to your father."

"Thanks, Mom," Micah said, grabbing his mom's hand to help her out the chair.

"I enjoyed our conversation," Cynthia said before turning to walk toward her husband.

"Me, too," Lex said with a smile. When she was alone with Micah, she rested her head on his shoulder, wishing that the conversation with his mother hadn't put her in such a sentimental mood. She loved hearing the love story, but she hated the affect the story was having on her. When she divorced Evan, she vowed to never get close to another man who could make her lose herself and become consumed by him. Everything about Micah was intoxicating in the most seductive way imaginable.

She lifted her head off his shoulder and pretended to observe her surroundings when in actuality, she wanted to steal glances at him. When he caught her eyes, they made her pause as if she hadn't seen his eyes before.

"I'm glad you're here," he said, his eyes remaining on hers and not on her lips where they usually ventured when he got her attention.

"I'm glad I'm here, too," she said, ignoring the chill that whipped in the air, twirling her scarf around her head. When she laid her head back on his shoulder, she was certain that Arkansas had a lot more in store for her. *Oh, well...there are way worse things to be consumed by than a man like Micah Madden.*

Chapter 11

Micah had no idea exactly what time it was, but if he had to guess, he would assume it was close to 3 a.m. The parade had been amazing and the time he'd spent with Lex had been even better.

After the parade, he'd introduced her to several towns-people who were close friends with his parents and informed them that he was planning a surprise anniversary party for them. As suspected, every person they spoke with was eager to attend and claimed it would be the biggest celebration in town history. When Lex's eyes landed on him questionably, he had to explain that not a lot happened in Cranberry Heights. Even marriages were few because a lot of couples found solace in Cranberry Heights after they married, while those raised here were eager to get out. It was a great town, but it had taken a hard hit after the economic downfall, leaving many future residents on a search to find something better. The winter festival was one of the few annual events that brought back old residents, new residents and tourists alike.

Although the day may have gone great, the night was an entirely different story. *This is ridiculous!* Micah thought as he discreetly glanced over at Lex. He knew she wasn't asleep, but she was adamant on pretending to be. When they got back to Madden Manor and retired to their room, Lex had gotten all antsy and jumpy. Last night, Micah had crept into the bedroom after Lex had fallen asleep and she had been sprawled on the bed snoring softly. She'd looked so cute and he didn't want to wake her, so he slept on the couch and was gone before she woke up.

Now, not only was she as quiet as a mouse and had been for the past two hours, she also hadn't moved a muscle. There was no way that wild sleeper from last night was the composed sleeper lying beside him in bed right now. They were separated by several oversize pillows and concealed under a soft velour cover, but he could still feel the heat between them lingering in the air, hiding under the sheets, and taunting his state of mind.

Damn! I feel like a horny-ass teenager. It was bad enough he was hard as hell with no signs of going down before sunrise. But even worse, he was lying still, not moving an inch, all because he knew she was doing the same damn thing. He'd been reduced to one of those lame men who shared beds with women they weren't sleeping with. *I can't do this every night...especially when she's within arms reach.*

Deciding to test his theory and see if she was really sleeping, he moved a couple inches toward the middle of the bed to see what she would do. Within seconds, she scooted a little more toward her edge of the bed. *Really? All this just to avoid being next to me?*

He moved another inch toward the middle of the bed, only this time he had to move halfway on the pillows that separated them. Just like the last time, Lex moved over closer to her edge of the bed. Micah mouthed an expletive and raised his hands in the air in disbelief before bringing them back down to his side. Tilting his head without raising his body, he glanced past the cover to see how much space she had left on the bed.

She's almost out of space, he concluded, deciding to cross over the pillow-drawn line in the center of the bed and enter Lex's sleeping territory.

Micah pushed on his forearms and lifted himself at the same time that Lex began sliding closer to the edge. His thigh brushed against her butt and in a frenzy, Lex scatted even farther to the brink of the bed until there was nowhere left to go but down.

"Shiitake mushrooms!" Lex yelped when her butt hit the floor…hard.

"Shi ti what?" Micah said as he bent over the bed to see if she was okay while trying to contain his laughter. Lex ignored his outreached hand and flew to her feet. The moonlight seeping through the curtain danced across her face, illuminating her features.

"Shiitake mushrooms," Lex repeated, readjusting her pajamas and denying Micah a free peep show. "I try not to swear so it's what I say in place of the *S* word."

Is she for real? Micah knew some women and men who preferred not to spit out curse words every second, but Lex was spurting out a word he'd never heard anyone use to replace a curse word.

"Good for you," Micah said still trying to contain his laughter.

"Shut up," Lex spouted as she pushed on his shoulders and thighs, trying to get him to move over to his side of the bed.

"What did I say?" he asked, playing the innocent role.

"You know darn well what I mean, Micah," she said still pushing him. "I can tell you want to laugh. I can hear it in your voice."

"So you say *shiitake mushrooms* in place of *shit* and you say *darn* instead of *damn?*" he asked, unable to resist taunting her.

"Shut up," she said again, pushing against his body even harder. "A lot of people say darn."

"I know. I'm just giving you a hard time. I like getting you all hot and bothered and this is the most your hands have been on me since we met."

Lex jumped back from the bed, and missed a step. "Fudgesicles," she shrieked, when she hit her foot on the bedpost. Her hand flew to her foot and she began hopping around in a half circle around the bedroom.

Micah threw himself back on the bed and released the hearty laugh he'd been trying to contain ever since Lex fell to the floor.

She shot him a dirty look before releasing her foot and wobbling back to the bed. He didn't miss the look of hurt on her face as she turned her back to him.

"I'm sorry," Micah said, reaching out for her arm. "I shouldn't laugh at your expense, but sometimes, you do the funniest things and I can't help but laugh."

"People laugh at me all the time," Lex said in a defeated voice. "Out of all of my close girlfriends, I get teased all the time because I'm a little clumsy."

I was supposed to be seducing her...not upsetting her. "I'm sorry, Lex," Micah said as he pulled her into his arms, taking note of how great she felt pressed against him. "I didn't think about how you would feel. I apologize for hurting your feelings, but you're unique and unlike any woman I've ever met. That's one of the reasons I'm so infatuated with you."

Her body began shaking uncontrollably. *Damn, I really messed this night up.* Just when he was about to apologize again, he heard her let out a chuckle. When she looked up at him, she was giggling...not crying.

"What the..." he said as it hit him she was joking around.

"Remember when you made me feel bad when we were walking to your car the other night back in Chicago," she said, sitting up in the bed. "Payback sucks doesn't it?"

"Payback, huh," he said, sitting upright. "I think the joke is really on you."

Her eyes twitched in confusion. "How so?"

"Well," Micah said drawling out the word while moving closer to Lex, "your mini performance gave me the opportunity to be next to you unlike I have before."

She gave him a skeptical look. "What do you mean?"

So glad you asked. "When you gave me the sad puppy-dog eyes, I was able to pull you into my arms, giving me the opportunity to feel your soft curves."

Her eyes softened, so he continued. "As I held you, I felt you relax in my arms...a sign that I'm growing on you."

"So, exactly how is the joke on me?"

"You don't get it, do you?" he asked with a slight chuckle. She shook her head to imply that she didn't.

"During that brief moment when you were trying to prank me, I had further decided that I wasn't going another night without tasting you again."

Micah placed both hands on either side of her thighs and pulled her into the center of his legs. She slid across the Egyptian cotton sheets with ease and her eyes widened in surprise and anticipation. The soft gasp that escaped her lips was barely audible. Her once mellow breathing now increased its pace. With one target on his mind, Micah's eyes zoomed in on her lips before pressing his mouth to hers.

It's been too long, he thought as he parted her mouth with his tongue and pulled her to him even closer. She only tensed for a moment before her body relaxed beneath his tender grasp and her mouth explored his with the same hunger. Micah vaguely remembered telling Lex that he would wait until she made the next move. But that was before he'd arrived in Arkansas and learned they would be sharing a room. Even so, he also knew giving her control was the validation he needed to kiss her and not feel guilty about it. Being so near her without touching her was absolute torture, but somehow, he convinced himself to listen to the more logical part of his brain and forced himself to stop kissing her.

"Sorry," Micah said, removing his hands from her hair, not remembering when his hands had even ventured to her hair in the first place. Their legs were tangled in the sheets, evidence that he'd still gotten more carried away than he'd planned.

He threw his head to the ceiling and puffed out a long breath before rotating his head to crack his neck and shifting his focus to Lex once more. After hours of lying in bed, he'd adjusted to seeing in the dark, so although her back was to the moonlight, he could read the question in her eyes.

"What are you questioning?" he whispered. "The fact that I kissed you?"

She slightly tilted her head to the side. "Actually," she said, brushing her tongue across her own lips. "I was curious why in the world you stopped…"

Gathering up as much courage as she could, Lex wrapped one hand around the back of Micah's head and pulled his lips back to hers. She pushed his back to the bed and straddled him, her lips never leaving his.

For years, she'd told herself that kissing a man the way she was kissing Micah was the type of kiss she could live without. *What was I thinking?* As their tongues mingled in the sweetest conversation, her hands roamed over his muscular arms slightly squeezing his biceps. He groaned at her touch and the erotic sound prompted her hands to continue their journey. She ventured under his shirt, finally able to touch his mouthwatering six-pack that she couldn't wait to see in daylight. She guessed the movement was what Micah had been waiting for because his hands that had been residing on her back, eased to her butt, fully cupping both cheeks.

"I knew you would fit perfectly in my palms," he said in between kisses. His words flowed through her like a cascade of water and elevated her desire. Slowly and seductively, she began rotating her hips, enjoying the feeling of him growing beneath her. Faint moans echoed in the room as they kissed, bit and sucked on each other's lips, both attacking one another with a starvation that food couldn't even satisfy.

In a quick move that caught her off guard, Micah

wrapped an arm around her waist and switched their position. He left a trail of wet kisses along her neck before moving to her breasts and delicately cupping them. He pushed her pajama shirt aside, a nipple escaping the constraints of the cotton fabric.

"Oh, my," Lex responded when his tongue grazed over one nipple while squeezing the other through the material. It had been way too long since her nipples had gotten any action, and Micah was definitely giving them the attention they deserved.

He left her breasts and lifted her shirt completely off, softly kissing her stomach and stopping at the drawstring of her pajama shorts.

"Lex," Micah said trying to get her to focus on him.

"Yes," she said as she lifted her head off the bed.

"Do you mind if I take these off?"

She briefly thought about the implication behind his request and what would come next if he removed her bottoms. She didn't take long to decide.

"Yes," she said, making sure she sounded confident. "You can take them off."

He gave her a sly smile before he undid the drawstring and slid the shorts off her. His hot fingers ran down her thighs followed by his daring tongue, each lick and touch hotter than the last. *What is he doing to me?* Lex was so wrapped up in the moment, she didn't feel him nudge her legs open until his tongue was on her center, lapping up her sweet juices.

She bucked off the bed giving Micah the opportunity to slide his hands under her butt, bringing her closer to his mouth. He dipped his tongue in and out of her core with determined precision, hitting her sweet spot with every lick. The ends of her toes curled into the sheets and her back lifted completely off the bed.

On their own accord, her hands gripped his face, not knowing if she should push him away or bring him even closer. When he plunged two fingers into her and encircled his mouth around her clit, her dilemma was forgotten. She gripped his head and held on for dear life as his long fingers played with her instrument while his mouth sang a sweet song in a way no man had ever done before.

Lex rolled her head to the ceiling and wailed a soft cry as she released an orgasm so strong she lost all sense of reality. Falling back to the bed, she closed her eyes, not believing that she'd been denied the sexual satisfaction of a man with a lethal mouth who knew how to please a woman.

"Shame on all the men who are too selfish to satisfy a woman in that kind of way," she said aloud, needing to voice the words for her own benefit, since until tonight she was one of those women.

"Told you I was the sweetest kind of troublemaker," Micah said, inching his way to her. He lay on his back and rolled her on top of him. Lex ran her fingers down his body with every intention of easing him inside her, when suddenly, he pulled her up by her thighs, stationing her center right above his mouth, the position forcing her on her hands and knees.

"We aren't having sex tonight," he said in the sexiest voice she'd heard yet. "But I do want to make you come as many times as possible."

She looked down between her legs to get a better view of him. The sight she saw nearly stole her breath. "Do you want me to lie back down?" she asked.

"No…just lower yourself onto my mouth," he said, still beneath her. "As if you're going to sit on my face."

Face sitting… She'd heard it was amazing from other women, but she never thought she'd have a man this irrefutably sexy asking her to willingly sit on his face. *I wish I could keep him in this position forever.* The thought made her close her eyes in embarrassment and surprise that she would even think such a thing. But Micah was daring her to live in the moment and had been since they had met.

Oh, my goodness, she thought as she spread her thighs more and slowly eased down onto his mouth. *This is really happening.* With each low movement, she could feel his warm breath teasing her wet center, anxiously awaiting the connection.

"Are you ready?" he asked in a deep raspy voice. She opened her mouth to tell him that she was, but the only word to escape was a pleasurable whimper of absolute satisfaction as his tongue dipped in her core and twirled around inside her.

Chapter 12

Lex slowly opened her eyes and glanced at the empty spot on the bed beside her. She briefly recalled Micah whispering in her ear that he had to get up early to assist with some activities at the festival and wouldn't be finished until 2 p.m. He seemed so involved in the community, and Lex would have never guessed that about him before visiting his family in Arkansas.

She took a long stretch and yawned before pushing the sheets and cover off her body. She was still naked, a sight that brought a small smile to her lips. Last night had been amazing and Lex couldn't believe that she'd willingly participated in such naughty behavior. She always attracted men who were all too eager to tell her how they could please her in the bedroom, and even if Lex had given those jerks the time of day, she knew that not one of them could have delivered the performance that Micah had last night.

Imagine how great he is in bed. She no longer wished to convince herself to stay away from Micah and she actually didn't think she could even if she tried. He wasn't just a sexy man, or a passionate man. He was a man who cared about pleasing her and put her needs before his own. She didn't want to think about Evan after such an amazing night, but she had to because being married to a man like him was what made her appreciate how Micah had handled her last night.

"Eeekk," she squealed as she kicked her legs in excitement. "What have you done to me, Micah Madden?" Not only did she feel like a new woman physically, but mentally, she felt relaxed and refreshed. *I guess it's true what they say,* she thought. *Orgasms really do relieve built-up tension.* She'd always thought it was a myth, but clearly she'd been wrong.

Lex stood up and gave her body another much-needed stretch, enjoying the freedom of being naked. You'd think living on her own she would've walked around naked every now and then, but she didn't. Right now, walking around naked until she showered and dressed for the day felt right.

She smirked to herself as she began singing one of her favorite holiday songs. She took it one step further and made up a dance to go along with her vocals. Gliding across the floor, she moved to the sound of her own voice, feeling more liberated than she had in a long time. She proudly hit the last note of the song, reminding herself that every woman should indulge in a little *me* time.

After her song, she went into the side drawer and got

out the clothes she would be wearing for the day along with her cosmetic bag.

"I much prefer you without any clothes on."

Lex yelped aloud and dropped everything she had in her hands at the sound of Micah's voice. Her hand flew to her heart as she swiftly turned around to find him standing in the doorway of the bathroom.

"What on earth are you still doing here?" Lex asked, oblivious to the fact that she was still naked. "You said you'd be busy until 2 p.m."

Micah gave her an amused look. "When was the last time you checked the clock?"

She looked over her shoulder at the clock on the nightstand. "Oh, wow, is it really 2:30?"

"It sure is, sunshine," he said, leaning against the wall wearing a white T-shirt and worn jeans. There were a few paint stains splattered on his clothes so she assumed whatever he did today included painting.

"I helped paint the inside foyer of the town hall," Micah said, reading her thoughts. Clearly captivated by Lex, his eyes perused her entire body with keen interest.

"But I'd much rather talk about how sexy you look and the fact that last night, I didn't notice how many cute brown freckles you had on your body."

"Oh, crap," Lex shrieked as she yanked the white sheet off the bed and covered her body. "Why didn't you say anything?" she asked as she began picking up the belongings that she'd dropped.

"I didn't know I had to remind you that you were naked," he said as he let out a robust laugh. "Plus I enjoyed watching you sing and dance. Your voice is amazing."

Although her family and close friends knew she could

sing, she rarely sang in front of them. "My parents placed me in voice lessons when I was younger," she told him. "Up until I was ten, I did voice-overs for numerous Chicagoland companies for different toys or musical books."

"You just keep amazing me lingerie girl," he said, moving toward her. "Did you mean what you said before you got out of bed?"

Lex raised an eyebrow at him when he reached her. *Got out of bed?* "Um, how long were you watching me?"

"Long enough to hear you say 'What have you done to me, Micah,'" he repeated in a girlie voice as he slightly flared his arms in the air.

"I did *not* sound like that," she said punching him in the arm. His eyes ventured to her hair and she figured she must look a complete mess. She brushed one hand over her disheveled hair before covering her mouth with the same hand.

"What are you doing?" Micah asked inquisitively.

"My hair is a mess and I still have morning breath."

"Seeing your hair like this let's me know that I did something right last night," he said with a wink. "And I don't mind morning breath." He removed her hand from her mouth.

"But I do," she said raising her hand back to her mouth. "And I had no idea I slept that long."

"I guess I'm to blame for that. We were up until 6 a.m."

"Did you even get any sleep?"

"Barely, and I don't have time for a nap either," he said. "Would you mind accompanying me to Little Rock today? I have a business dinner there with a potential investor and they are bringing their wives."

Kinda like a date?

"I'll go. How far is Little Rock?"

"Um, with the way I drive, it's about two hours…not too far," he answered before removing her hand again and glancing at her lips.

"Hold that thought," she said when he started leaning in to kiss her. She went to the bathroom and brushed her teeth, trying to ignore the fact that he was watching her do so and was blocking the door so she couldn't close it.

"So after last night I guess privacy is out of the question?" she asked in between brushing.

"Pretty much," he said with a smile as he brushed his hands over his goatee and looked her up and down. That was another quality that she really liked about him. Despite the fact that she was sure she looked like a swamp creature with her hair all crazy and her lips swollen from kisses, he still looked at her as if she was the most beautiful woman he'd ever seen. Given that he was such a good-looking man, she knew he attracted beautiful women all the time and she was sure they were those type of women who would never let a man see them in this state.

"Why do you like me?" she asked, walking past him to the bedroom.

"Why wouldn't I like you?"

"What exactly do you like?"

"What is there not to like?"

She twisted her mouth to the side. "Why am I really in Arkansas?"

"Why do you think you're in Arkansas?"

She placed one hand on her hip and turned to him. "Why do you keep answering my questions with a question?"

He took a step forward, stopping centimeters from her face. "Why are you asking me so many questions?"

"Because I really want to know," she said sincerely, her voice barely above a whisper.

Instead of responding, he closed the distance and gently placed his lips on hers. Her unanswered questions were forgotten, as she got lost in his intoxicating taste.

On the drive to Little Rock, Lex and Micah had given Cyd and Shawn a call to see how plans were going for the wedding. Micah was excited for his friend to finally marry a woman who understood him and loved him as fiercely as he loved her. When his brother Malik had first introduced him to Shawn, they'd hit it off instantly. Although they'd matured into respectable men and dedicated their lives to the safety of others, both had gone through a bad-boy streak that some may argue was still part of their personality.

Now Micah and Lex were sitting in his parents' Highlander in comfortable silence.

"I want to make a pit stop before we get downtown," he said to her, never taking his eyes off the road. There was so much more about him that he wanted her to know and understand.

"Okay," she responded. "Are you going to tell me where?"

"I want it to be a surprise," he said, preferring to see her reaction to the location when they arrived.

Twenty minutes later, they entered a part of the city east of downtown, where Micah had spent most of his childhood. As they drove through the low-income neighborhood, he noticed Lex tense. She was always full of questions so he figured she had questions now, but for some reason, she didn't say anything.

They passed several corners that were filled with young

men either hanging out with nothing to do, or discreetly selling drugs. Although Micah hadn't been around the old neighborhood in years, he still felt comfortable in his original hometown.

When they arrived on his old block, Micah shook his head thinking about how much his family's lifestyle had changed after they moved to Cranberry Heights.

"Here we are," Micah said as he pulled over in front of a small boarded-up home.

Lex glanced at the house before setting her eyes on him. "What did you want to show me?"

"This is it," he said pointing to the house. "This is the home I grew up in."

Her eyes widened as she turned back to the house. "How long did you and your family live here?"

"Until I was sixteen," Micah said. "My mom and dad had moved here back when the neighborhood wasn't as bad as it is today. My dad grew up in the area and was the director of a community center six blocks away. My mom taught at the elementary school that was right next door so they both chose to live close to their jobs."

"That makes sense," she replied.

"It did," Micah said. "My mom took off work for a while when she began having children, but she remained a substitute teacher."

"Are you the second oldest after Malik? Your mom mentioned that she had six sons. I knew you had brothers, but I had no idea there were six of you."

"You guessed right. Malik and I are less than two years apart," he said. "My brother Malakai was born after me, followed by fraternal triplets, Crayson, Caden and Carter."

"Oh, my goodness! Your mom didn't mention triplets.

That's nuts! I like the *M* and *C* name combo, though," she said with a laugh. "Was that done purposely?"

"You catch on quick, Turner," he said, joining in her laughter. "Before we were all born, my parents had decided if they had boys, their names would begin with *M* like my dad's. If they had girls, their names would begin with *C* like my mom's. Years after having three sons, my mom wanted to try for a girl and convinced my dad to have one more child. To both of their surprise, they were informed they were having triplets. Neither one of them was prepared for the news since natural reproduction of triplets was so rare. But my dad is a twin, so he was less surprised than my mom. Giving up her hope of having a girl, she gave the triplets names that begin with the letter *C*."

"Your mom is a warrior," she said with a smile.

"She is and I love her for it," he agreed, turning his head at the sound of a garbage can falling over due to a stray cat.

"What about your dad? Raising six sons could not have been easy."

"It wasn't," he said. "Especially when you have a son like me who was constantly getting in trouble."

"How so?"

Micah turned in the driver's seat to face her. "Growing up in this neighborhood can be hard for a young man trying to come into his own. Malik was known as the intelligent brother. Malakai was the creative one. And the triplets are years younger than Malakai so they were just developing their individual personalities. Me on the other hand…I had the street smarts."

Micah glanced at the front window, the white fog slowly overtaking the entire glass. "Since my mom was a teacher, she made sure we all studied as much as possible. I guess you can say I was born smart because I rarely studied, but I always got good grades. In my adolescence, my boredom resulted in me pranking teachers, spray painting the sides of buildings, and pickpocketing tourists downtown."

"Please tell me you did not steal from people," Lex exclaimed.

"I never stole anything big, but the friends I had growing up convinced me that stealing from people who had money, wasn't stealing."

"You mean like Robin Hood."

"Something like that," he said with a laugh. "Any money I took I usually spent on food for people in the neighborhood who didn't have enough to eat. I wasn't thinking about the consequences back then because all I knew was that I wanted to give back to the community in some type of way. School bored me, girls bored me and, quite frankly, life in general bored me."

"What else did you get into?" she inquired.

"What didn't I get into…" Micah turned back to face her. "When I became a teenager, I learned that I could survey a situation and come up with a solution instantly. I didn't just have sales skills. I knew how to strategize and create different tactics that delivered results. I didn't want to do anything reckless like sell drugs or get into gambling, so instead I decided to put my skills to use in another way."

"Like what?" she asked with interest as she shifted in her seat.

"I began discreetly following around some of the drug dealers in the area who all worked for the same leader. I observed the way they interacted with others in their group and enemies from neighboring areas. After about a month of following around some of the biggest dealers in my neighborhood, I approached one of them who I knew from school and asked him to set up a meeting with his boss and I."

"You've got to be kidding me," she said, resting her head on the headrest. "Why would you set up a meeting with the head drug dealer?"

"To tell him what his organization was lacking. I told him that although he was running a good system, he could be running it much smoother. I gave him a strategy plan on how to increase his sales and reduce the number of killings in the area. The plan also included a way to have a less violent relationship with enemies."

If Micah could think of one word to describe Lex's face, *astounded* was the first word that came to mind. He expected her to be surprised, but he needed her to know that being who he was in the past molded him in a positive way, although what he had done back in the day weren't his most shining moments. Her mouth opened, and he held his breath to see what she would say. "So… you helped drug dealers sell more drugs?" she asked.

Chapter 13

Helped drug dealers sell more drugs? "In a way, I guess I did," he said. "But my main goal when I constructed my plan was trying to reduce the number of killings in Little Rock. So in my mind, I figured I would go to the source and create a plan to do that. I never thought about the consequences, I only thought about my main goal."

She searched his eyes, and Micah tried his best not to fidget under her scrutinizing observation. He turned down the heat in the SUV, growing hotter under her gaze. He really didn't share his past with too many people, but he'd decided a while ago that he wanted a future with Lex, so he needed to be honest with her.

"I've never told this story to another woman," he said, unable to take the silence any longer. "In order to understand the man I became, I wanted to tell you about the man I used to be, no matter how stupid the decisions were I made in my past."

She was quiet for a moment longer before she squinted her eyes together. "You say that like you believe I think you're a bad person after hearing the story," she finally stated.

"Not a bad person," he said. "But I do recognize that I didn't always make the best decisions and I have to live with that."

"How long did you help that drug dealer?"

"For a few years, only when they needed a new strategy," Micah said, letting out a deep breath. "The killings in the neighborhood did reduce 20 percent from previous years, but I think my parents knew I was doing something I shouldn't have. Like I said earlier, I maintained good grades, so my relationship with them was fine until a terrible fire destroyed the community center and the school. Both my parents lost their jobs."

"Oh, no," she said as her hands rushed to her chest. "What did your parents do?"

"My mom started substitute teaching at another school and my dad began working odd jobs. Malik and I were both working at a local grocery store, so we handed over our checks to our parents to help with the mortgage and our brothers. Although Malakai wasn't old enough to work a real job, he began selling his artwork to shops downtown."

"That was really responsible of the three of you," she said, lowering her hands to her lap. "If they didn't know exactly what you were doing, what strained your relationship?"

His jaw twitched at the memory and he turned to stare out the foggy front window again. "My dad got into an altercation with the dealer I was helping when he saw him unnecessarily rough up another man pretty bad. I happened to be with my dad and told him to stay out of it, but my dad wanted to make sure the guy was okay. When the dealer confronted him, I was able to clear up the confusion and get him to step off my dad. But my dad wasn't stupid. He asked me about my relationship with the guy, so I fessed up, tired of hiding the truth."

Lex reached between them and lightly placed her hand on his. The gesture made him return his focus on her. "My mom and my brothers were disappointed in me, but when I told them I was changing my ways, they began to forgive me. My dad, on the other hand, was a different story. My uncle Barry, who lived in Cranberry Heights, found out the town was in need of a community director and contacted my dad. He interviewed right away and got the job. We all uprooted to Cranberry Heights, and the town was so impressed with my dad that within years, the townspeople suggested that he run for mayor."

"I had no idea your dad was mayor," she said with surprise.

"He was until a few years ago," Micah stated. "He fell into the position years ago after my uncle, who was mayor at the time, was killed in a car accident. My dad was chosen as the interim mayor and the position became permanent. When my parents decided to open up a B and B in town, they devoted all their focus on that, and my dad decided not to run for mayor anymore."

"I'm so sorry to hear about your uncle."

"Thanks," he said. "It was hard at the time, but that was a long time ago."

She searched his eyes with curiosity before asking the question he knew was coming. "So, why is your relationship with your dad still strained?"

Micah shook his head at the thought. "When we moved,

I still maintained contact with a few friends that I've had over the years. They weren't all dealers, but some of them weren't good people either. My closest friend at the time was the worst, and my dad warned me to stay away from him. He had thought that moving from Little Rock and me getting accepted into Fisk University in Tennessee would finally allow me to shake off those bad relationships. But instead, I convinced myself that my dad had forgotten where he came from, and I wasn't going to be that person."

He briefly paused as he continued to reminisce about his past. "While that friend was visiting me in college, something serious happened that caused me to eventually transfer out of the school. I later found out that him and his boys were reckless everywhere they went. That's when I realized that it wasn't enough to just be a good person. You had to surround yourself by good people and I had been hanging around all the wrong people."

Her eyes crooked in inquiry. "Is that when you were arrested?"

"The one and only time," he replied, still irritated with himself. "The case was dropped based on false accusations, but the damage to my relationship with my dad was done. Our relationship has been tense ever since."

"What happened to get you arrested?"

Micah stretched in his seat. "Let's save that for another conversation," he said, brushing his hand against her chin. "Just know that I'm a different man than I once was." *And I desperately need you to believe me.* She glanced out the window before glancing at him. The expression on her face was unreadable.

Lex watched a range of emotions cross Micah's face while he talked about his past. From the short time she'd spent with his family, she really enjoyed being around them. And in a way, hearing Micah recap his past only made her respect his family more.

"Can I ask one last question and then we can change the subject?" she asked.

"Shoot," he said confidently, although she read the hesitation in his eyes.

"How did you become a police officer?"

"After I transferred schools, I finally understood my purpose. I'd grown out of the thuggish days and decided to pursue a career helping others…mainly young men. I wanted a fresh start and I figured going to school in the Midwest would be a nice change. I double majored in Criminal Justice and Computer Science and graduated from Michigan State University in three years by taking classes every summer. The week before graduation, I was encouraging students to go to college at my old high school and was approached by the Little Rock chief of police about enlisting in the police academy. I thought it was a great way to make a difference in my old neighborhood, so I took a shot at it."

"That's so great," she said.

"It was," he agreed. "I was one of the best cops at my station and things were going great, until I realized there were more dirty cops than good cops in my unit so I put in a request to transfer. Malik and Shawn both knew each other from their FBI days, so when Shawn heard about my dilemma, he told me about his dream to open his own security company. I knew it was the break I'd been waiting for so I quit my job and teamed up with Shawn."

As she sat there, completely indulged in Micah's story, she realized that it wasn't just his story that intrigued her. It was him as a man. The way he thought. The goals he had. The way he made her feel. If she wasn't careful, she would fall head over heels in love with him. She no longer knew if falling for him was a bad or a good thing, but what she did know was that being vulnerable to a man made her nervous.

Worry lines were visible on his forehead and she realized that he was waiting to hear her response to his story. Usually, his eyes would roam over her lips and her body, but this evening, he was different. His eyes remained on hers, waiting for acceptance and understanding.

"You certainly have many layers, Micah Madden," she said softly as she turned in her seat so that her back was now pressed against the door. "You're a great man. Your story is part of what made you who you are, and just as you told me, your experiences have made you stronger not weaker. I admire your determination to help young men figure out that they have options."

"The world is theirs to conquer," he added, giving her a smile of relief for the first time since they'd arrived in his old neighborhood.

He's so cute. Looking at her with gleeful eyes, he looked every bit of sixteen sitting across from her, rather than the thirty-year-old man that he was. He glanced at the clock before turning the heat back up.

"Are you ready for dinner?"

"Let's go," she stated, turning back around and buckling her seat belt. "Thanks for bringing me here and sharing your story," she said once they'd started driving.

He flashed her a million-dollar grin. "Thank you for listening to my story with an open mind."

The conversation with the wives of the investors had been entertaining. Halfway through dinner, Micah had winked at her, a sign they had agreed he would give if the dinner meeting was going well. By the time they all said their goodbyes, there was talk about finalizing a contract, and a promise that Micah would bring Lex along for the next dinner. Grant and Parker were a huge account and she was so proud of Micah for representing his company so well. They made a good team, and tonight they'd put on a performance better than most seasoned couples.

"This was so much fun," she said to Micah as she removed her peacoat, keeping her eyes straight ahead on the road as they headed back to Cranberry Heights. He'd removed his coat thirty minutes ago and ever since he did, all she could think about was running her hands up and down his hazelnut abs. She squeezed her legs closer together. *Lex Turner! You know better! You can control your emotions.* Her encouraging thoughts weren't helping. Her panties were drenched…a situation she had *never* been in before.

"I'm glad you had a good time," he said, his eyes leaving the road to glimpse at her. She told herself not to glance back at him, but she couldn't help it. She turned her head to look at him and quickly turned back to the road before she reached his eyes. There was no doubt in her mind that she'd be even more uncomfortable during the car ride if she looked at his face. *His sexy face… masculine jawline…neatly groomed goatee…sop them up with biscuit lips.* She shook her head to clear her mind. *Look at the road, Lex. Straight ahead. Into the dark. Not Micah's creamy hazelnut complexion.* Her head slowly turned toward Micah again. *No, wrong way. Look outside,* she reminded herself, causing her to whip her head back forward.

"I got you," she said aloud, frustrated that her mind and body weren't listening to each other.

"Are you okay," he asked glancing from her to the road.

"Yup," she answered quickly, remaining in her same position.

"Are you sure?"

"Sure am."

"Absolutely positive?" he asked.

"Indeed."

They passed a large sign stating they were close to Cranberry Heights, followed by a highway sign with restaurants and gas stations on it. "Mind if I make a stop?" he questioned.

"Go right ahead."

"Do you want some dessert?"

"Sure. Why not." *Now who's asking all the questions!*

"What are you in a mood for?"

"You," she said breathlessly as she dropped her head to her hands, tired of answering all his questions. "Just you." She finally looked over at him, not caring that her desire was on display. He searched her eyes, remaining silent for a moment.

"I thought so," he finally said with a smirk, turning back to the road. *Of course he knew.* It seemed lately, he knew how she felt before she even knew how she felt.

"Well, now you know," she voiced in irritation, leaning her head on the seat. She was more aggravated by her lack of self-control than his accurate assessment of her yearnings.

"Then I guess we better fix that," he stated, yanking the car over a lane and hopping off at the next exit.

"That sign said there were a least a couple more stops until we got to our exit."

"I know," he said, driving like a bat out of hell. He turned off the main road onto a narrow gravel road with meadows on either side that rose taller than the car.

"If this is the time when you confess that you're really a serial killer, I only ask that you kill me quickly." Because of the bumpy road, she had a tight grip on one of the door rests while her other hand gripped her seat.

"I'm not a serial killer, but I should tell you now that I can't be held responsible for my actions," he responded, looking in her direction for the first time since he jumped off the expressway. "Because the wicked things I want to do to you are definitely illegal."

Good. God. Almighty. His stimulating words kissed every part of her sensual body. She threw back her head, thinking the best thing to do in this situation was pray to the goddess of love. Closing her eyes and clasping her hands together, she prayed.

"Dear lover goddess, please endorse the sins I am about to partake in. I know not what is right, for all I want to do is wrong," she reached her hands in the air before bringing them back together. "For tonight, I ask that you give me the stamina to sustain all that I can, the courage to let all my inhibitions go, and the ability to twist my body in ways inhumanly possible. For tonight, I allow myself to go to a place I've never gone before," she peeked one eye open to find that the car had stopped in front of an old house. "Amen."

"Amen," Micah said in a raspy voice. "I don't know whether I should be on high alert because you just said a prayer before we make love or if I should say a prayer, too, because listening to you made me feel dirty."

In one swift move, he lifted her off the seat and onto his lap. "Truthfully, the only thing your love request made me want to do is get you naked as soon as possible and have my way with you."

In that moment, she realized she'd been waiting her entire life for a man to make her feel this way…for a man to truly get her. She felt special. Desired. Appreciated. "Then what are you waiting for."

Chapter 14

Micah couldn't move fast enough. He opened the door and stepped out with Lex in his arms. He didn't place her on her feet until he got to the porch to open the front door. He knew he had to act fast and turn on the lights before she got spooked. After all, they were in the middle of nowhere.

He found the light switch and flipped on the living room light. He rushed over to two heaters and put them on, then turned on a lamp so he could cut the main lights back off. He wanted the lighting to be as intimate as possible.

"Does anyone live here?" she asked as he pulled down the Murphy bed and pulled covers and sheets from the closet.

"Not yet," he said as he tried his best to place the covers on the bed. "The owners moved out nine months ago and I bought the place."

Her eyes grew bigger. "You plan on moving back to Arkansas?"

"No," he said, laughing at her expression. "I plan on fixing it up and renting her out. I own a property in Little Rock, too, that I would have showed you if we had time."

"You're full of surprises, aren't you," she said coming from behind him and wrapping her arms around his back while he made the bed. It was finally warming up in the room. Either that, or he was getting heated from her touch.

Her arms wrapped around him felt so right. She felt right. Even in this unfurnished house, *they* felt right. Micah turned around to face her. He never would have thought the woman looking at him now was the same woman who'd walked into the lingerie shop several months ago. The woman he'd met that day had been innocent, cute, endearing and a little bit clumsy. And even then, he'd been intrigued by her. But the woman staring back at him tonight was an entirely different one. Tonight, she was confident, captivating and downright sexy.

She bit her bottom lip before slipping her tongue in and out of her mouth. When her tongue slid back out of her mouth, he crushed his lips to hers. Her sweet moans filled the air around them and encouraged him to take the kiss deeper, exploring her mouth from one side to the other.

She stopped kissing him to remove her boots. He imitated her actions and removed his, too. Deciding to waste no more time, he pulled her sweater over her head, eagerly tugging down her leggings, as well. Her hands flew to his button-up, gently undoing the first couple buttons before standing on her tiptoes to yank the shirt over his head. When her hands moved to his pants, he stopped her and removed them himself.

"If your hands go anywhere near that area, this will be over before it starts," he huffed in a rushed breath. His voice sounded strained even to his own ears. A clear sign that he had to have her tonight. Right now.

He took a moment to stand back and observe her lacy bra and panty set. Although he'd seen her naked last night and this morning, this was the first time she allowed him the benefit to look as he pleased. He briefly studied her face to make sure his blatant appraisal of her wasn't making her nervous. He was satisfied that her eyes mirrored the lust reflected in his own. "You're absolutely breathtaking," he told her, vocalizing the words floating around in his mind.

From day one, he'd known he wanted her even if she hadn't wanted to acknowledge the fact. Now, her look solidified her acceptance of the intimate step they were taking in their relationship.

With two snaps of his fingers, her bra fell to the floor, followed by her panties. He lifted her from the floor and gently placed her in the middle of the bed, before standing straight to remove his boxers. Her eyes burned a hole in him as she watched in anticipation, her breasts rising and falling steadily. When he popped free of the confining cotton, her stunned gasp filled the room.

"You're beautiful," she said in a seductive, tone. *Beautiful?* He wasn't sure if a woman had ever called him beautiful before. And even if a woman had called him that, he was sure they never looked as sexy as Lex did stretched out naked awaiting his arrival.

Slowly, Micah eased himself onto the bed, bringing his lips to her face as he did. In gradual, circular movements, his tongue traveled across her neck, branding her caramel skin in a way he knew no man had ever done before. When he hit a tender part of her neck, her body lifted off the bed in response to the pleasure.

"Told you I'd have you spread-eagle style on my bed," he whispered in her ear.

"You're so cocky."

"And you like that about me," he said, rewarded by her passionate smile.

"Please don't make me wait, Micah," she begged.

Not one to be told twice, he reached down on the side of the bed and pulled a condom out of his wallet. After protecting them both, he hovered over her and resumed the journey his lips had started moments prior.

When both their moans increased to a level of pure euphoria, he joined them in the most intimate way possible in one provocative thrust.

"Ah," he groaned in satisfaction, already warning himself to hold on for as long as he could. She was wet. Tight. Slick. His mouth was already well acquainted with her taste, and now his cock was getting familiar with her inner walls.

He threw his head to the ceiling as he rhythmically pumped in and out of her. She placed her hands on his butt cheeks, sucking him in even deeper as she met him thrust for thrust.

"What are you doing to me," she said breathlessly. Earlier that morning he'd heard her say those same words to herself when she hadn't known he was in the bathroom. Now, hearing her say them for him to hear caused him to swell even more inside her.

"Oh, my…" she screamed, evidently feeling him getting bigger…thicker. "I'm close, Micah. Real close…"

"Me, too," he said, concluding that sex with Lex was different than any women he'd ever had intercourse with. That fact made him increase his pumps, needing to relieve them both of the tension building in their bodies.

He kneeled on the bed, never disconnecting them and placed both palms on each of her thighs. "Wrap your legs around my waist," he instructed her as he pulled her thighs onto his so that she was sitting on his lap. Lex obeyed, and when she was securely in place, he grabbed her by her hips and began lifting her up and down, quickly sliding her in and out. It took him a few seconds to register the animal-like growl that escaped his own mouth. Soon, his growl was joined by her feline purr as both sounds mingled in the air resulting in the sweetest love music that Micah had ever heard.

Without further warning, his body jerked in release at the same time he felt her convulse uncontrollably in his arms. Completely and utterly spent, they both collapsed on the bed, only gathering enough strength to look at one another and smile. The satisfaction was evident on both of their faces, neither able to formulate any words. *Words aren't necessary,* he thought as he pulled her into his arms and continued to soak in the moment.

You've got to think of a better lie, Lex thought to herself as she wobbled from one food table to the next. Being a foodie, Lex had been really excited to help Micah's family pass out chili dishes and taste all the different Southern cuisines that had entered the Warm Your Soul food competition. Now that she was here, she really wished she would have listened to Micah and soaked in the tub before they left.

She glanced across the room at Micah and his mom

as they passed out bowls of her famous white bean and turkey chili. He caught her eye and winked before greeting some more customers. Lex was initially helping them pass out the chili, but her legs had started cramping up, so Micah had advised her to walk around and try to stretch.

Last night, they'd made love more times than she could count and Lex hadn't really thought about the fact that she hadn't had sex in over six years. She'd been too wrapped up in the moment to think about the sad sex life she'd subjected herself to after her divorce. She also hadn't gotten a chance to tell Micah how long it had been since she was sexually active. She had a feeling he knew it had been a while, but she was sure that if he'd known she'd been celibate for over 2,190 days, it would have ruined the moment.

"Hi, miss," said a cheerful lady with a Southern drawl and a bright red Christmas sweater on. "Want to try some of my famous five-layer mac and cheese?" she asked, handing Lex a plate.

"Thank you," she responded, taking the dish from the lady. *So much for my winter diet,* she thought as she took a bite of the deliciously cheesy pasta. There wasn't one dish that she'd tasted that she didn't like, with the exception of a chitlins-and-rice dish that she couldn't stomach after one whiff.

"This is delicious," she told the woman as she turned to walk to another table.

"Are you okay," the lady asked Lex. "You're walking mighty funny."

"I guess yoga isn't for everyone," Lex responded with a laugh, sticking with her original lie. Anything was better than saying she had the best sex of her life last night, and now she couldn't walk straight.

"Oh, I agree," the mac-and-cheese lady said, clasping her hands together. "I once went to a yoga class they had in the high school gym, and by the time we got to the downward dog, I prepared to do the move and couldn't get up. Is that what happened to you?"

"Um," Lex said, trying to come up with a response. "Yeah. The downward dog is the same move that put me in this position." When she thought about all the different ways Micah had bent her legs, they'd definitely done something similar to the downward dog, so she was at least telling the woman part of the truth.

"Well, when you get home. Take a nice bath," the lady suggested.

"Thanks! I'll do that," Lex said before making her way back to Micah and Cynthia. When she got to the table, she placed the remaining mac and cheese on the table and took a picture of it so she could upload the image on her Instagram account along with the picture she'd taken of herself eating a bowl of Cynthia's chili earlier.

"Are you enjoying yourself?" Cynthia asked.

"I'm having a great time," Lex responded with a smile. She glanced over in time to see Micah take a swig of his water, looking at her over the bottle. She tried to will her eyes away, but she couldn't, mesmerized by the way his throat constricted when he swallowed.

"Sweetie," Cynthia said after she passed a dish to another customer. "Are you okay? I noticed you've been limping all morning."

She pulled her eyes away from Micah. "I hurt myself practicing a yoga move last—I mean, this morning."

Micah slightly choked on his water, but she refused to look at him.

Cynthia lifted an eyebrow. "You did all that," she said,

pointing a finger at Lex's legs. "What type of pose did this to you?"

"Ummm…the downward dog," she replied, saying the first thing that came to mind. In her peripheral view, she saw Micah turn away, probably to keep himself from laughing in front of his mother. *Stay calm,* Lex warned herself, knowing that if she got flustered, she would blush. And Micah's mom was already paying close attention to her.

Lex looked to the floor before stealing a peek at Micah, who was still turned away from them.

"Oh, I see," Cynthia said, looking from Lex to Micah. "Downward dog, huh? That must have been some yoga move." With that, she smiled at Lex before assisting more customers.

"How embarrassing. Way to help me out," Lex whispered as she punched Micah in the arm when his mom wasn't looking.

"Yoga?" Micah said with a laugh. "LG, I couldn't help you with that one. And I told you to take a bath this morning when we snuck back into the manor."

"I know," she said with a pout. "And now I'm paying the price. My thighs are killing me."

"Well," he said, wrapping his arms around her waist. "How about we leave here in thirty minutes, I run you a nice hot bath and then we head back downtown for a couple night festivities."

"Hmm…like an official date?" she said, wrapping her arms around his neck.

"Yes, an official date," he answered. "Plus, I need you good to go for the Snowlympics the day after tomorrow since you're my partner for the events."

She looked at him inquisitively. "Do I even want to know what Snowlympics is? It sounds intense."

"You'll find out soon enough," he replied. "I'm just helping you fulfill my proposition to be more spontaneous."

"I assume that's what last night was about, too, right?" she responded, placing a quick kiss on his mouth. "And the night before?"

"Now you're getting it," he said before giving her a kiss that caught the eyes of a few onlookers.

Chapter 15

He was falling for her. Hard. Quick. And although he knew she was different from the moment he met her, the feeling was still something he wasn't used to. Their date last night had been perfect, and now all he could think about was a life filled with plenty more moments like that one.

"Earth to Micah," Lex said, snapping her fingers in front of his face. "Did you hear what I said?"

No...I was too busy looking at your face...lips... breasts...eyes. "Micah," she said again when he'd dazed back off. "Since the Snowlympics is tomorrow and the Christmas party at the B and B is after that, I need you to focus. Here are the plans I have for your parents' 35th anniversary party so far." She slid her notebook to him.

The current mayor had let them utilize the town hall. They'd been sitting in an unoccupied conference room for two hours as he handled some necessary M&M Security paperwork, while she made calls to the Elite Events office and other vendors she needed to assist with the party. Micah had also called his brothers and his cousins and learned that a couple of them couldn't make it to Arkansas for New Year. They had then decided to plan the surprise anniversary party in early February instead, so that everyone could make it.

"Okay," Lex said, pointing to one of the items on her list. "I'll talk to Mr. Grudy to make sure he is okay with us throwing the anniversary party at his barn house. It's the only place large enough to hold 300 to 400 people, so I think it will be perfect."

"Sounds good. He'll be fine with it and the more I think about it, maybe I should tell my parents that Mr. Grudy is throwing a Cranberry Heights Founder's Day party since the town was founded in February. That way they won't suspect anything if word gets around town."

"That would be great," she agreed. "Also, here is a list of the food dishes and desserts that will be available, all being supplied by shops here in town. We are outsourcing the cake and having it brought here from a bakery in Little Rock, a suggestion from the bakery here since this event is so special."

"I'm fine with that. What about the decorations?"

"All under control," she said, taking out her laptop. She typed in a few keys and turned her computer toward Micah. "Here are some images of the decor I have in mind after really studying your parents and taking note of their individual styles."

Micah liked the decoration ideas immediately. Victorian lace and old-world embellishments representing his mom, combined with charming rustic designs themed around nature that represented his dad.

"I love it," he said with a smile. "What website is this?"

She lifted her eyebrows. "You've never been on Pinterest?"

"Um, what exactly is Pinterest?"

"Oh, man," she said as she hit the backspace button on her computer. "Here's my Pinterest homepage. It's basically a site that allows you to electronically pin things you love to themed user boards. That way, all your likes are in one place in whatever category you want."

He laughed at the excited look on her face. "So I guess it's the same as cutting out pics from magazines, right?"

"True," she said turning the computer back to her and scrolling to another page. "But it's way more effective. I created a secret board for your parents' anniversary party that only my partners and I have access to. That's the electronic board I was in when I showed you the decor images."

"Pinterest. Instagram. I'm learning a lot about you Lex."

"Like what?" she asked.

"Like the fact that you're a visualizer and you need to visualize things to see the bigger picture. You probably react better to people and places after you do a little research through a website or social media," he said. "Am I right?"

"You don't know me," she said with a giggle that let him know he was right. "I'm just glad you like my ideas so far."

"I do. And I know my mom will be so surprised.

There's no way she'd think her sons or even her nieces came up with this decor."

"What about your dad?" Lex asked, gathering her notes to stack them in a neat pile.

"He'll probably be excited until he realizes that it was my idea to throw them a surprise anniversary party."

"Have you ever talked to your dad about how he makes you feel?"

"I gave up trying to talk to him," he huffed. "Years ago, after that college incident, my dad decided that I wasn't worth his time."

"I don't think that's true," Lex chimed in. "Every time I see you and your dad together, you both look like you want to say more, but don't."

"If he wanted to say something to me, he would."

"Or," Lex said gently, rubbing his hand, "like you, your father is stubborn and doesn't know how to right a wrong. I'm sure he was mad at you back then, but I bet he got over it and was just too proud to apologize."

Long ago, Micah had decided that he couldn't care about his dad's opinion of him. "When I needed a father most, he turned his back on me. If it weren't for my uncle Barry, who knows how I would have turned out."

"Son," Cynthia Madden said, entering the conference room, "I didn't know you felt this way and I probably should have had this conversation with you years ago."

Micah's head shot over to Lex, and he was glad to see that she had closed her laptop and placed all of the party planning documents back in her bag.

"What are you doing here?" he asked.

"I had to drop off some papers for the town-hall council meeting tonight. I didn't know you two were here."

"We're catching up on work," Micah said. "What conversation should you have had with me?"

Cynthia took a seat next to Micah. "Growing up, your father was constantly in trouble. It seemed he couldn't stay out of it. Even when he met me, he was still running up and down the streets of Arkansas. Believe it or not, what you went through was nothing compared to the things your father did."

Micah shook his head in disbelief. "Naw, I don't believe that. Dad has always been big in the community and into doing the right thing. Cranberry even chose him as mayor."

"But he wasn't always like that," Cynthia said. "I loved him and tried to convince him to give up a life in the streets when we met, but eventually I had to accept him for the man he was and I couldn't change that. Your uncle even tried convincing us to move to Cranberry Heights years before we actually did. But Mason chose to change his ways when he found out I was pregnant with Malik. The day we found out, your dad drove out here to Cranberry and told your uncle that he was going to stop being reckless and start a better life for his family. Luckily, people in Little Rock believed in him and he was given that community director job."

What? Micah couldn't believe what his mom was telling him. For years, he'd assumed that his father didn't understand what he went through back in Little Rock when, actually, he understood all too well.

"You know what I think," Lex said, still rubbing her hands against his, "I think that before our trip is over, you should have a conversation with your dad. A real conversation."

"I agree," Cynthia said giving her son a soft smile.

Micah looked from one woman to the other, trying to push aside years of anger and resentment to focus on the overall picture. Life was too short. If the streets had taught him anything, that was definitely it.

"Okay," Micah finally stated. "Before we leave, I'll talk to Dad."

"Great," Lex said with a gleeful smile. "I think the conversation will go well."

Micah smiled but kept the rest of his thoughts to himself. Conversations with his dad never went well.

"I can't believe we were in the town hall for four hours," Micah said, running his long fingers over his face. Although it was chilly outside and the first December snow had fallen, Lex had suggested that they take the thirty-minute walk back to Madden Manor instead of waiting for the local bus to arrive, which they'd taken to get into town.

"The life of an event planner," she said with a laugh. "Plus, we hadn't planned on running into your mom. On a positive note, I shouldn't have to bug you with any more details. I can handle everything from this point on, now that I have all your family's contact info. Patty in the library said she can print off the invites for all the townsfolk tonight so I can hand those out tomorrow since you aren't limiting who can come from here."

"That's good to know," he replied as they walked side by side down the long road to the house. "I don't know how I let you talk me into taking the bus this morning instead of driving. And now we're walking home in the cold," he said with a chuckle.

"I want to soak in as much of Cranberry as I can before we leave," she said, no longer surprised that she'd grown to love the town. "Besides. It's not that cold and I love looking at the fresh-fallen snow blanketed over the hills."

She could feel Micah's eyes on her, so she turned to look back at him. "What?" she asked.

"This doesn't have to be a one-time trip," he said to her. "Even though we head back to Chicago soon, I'd like to bring you back here sometime."

"I'd like that," she said, slipping her hand in his. The gesture had become natural to them, and when they weren't holding hands, Lex felt like something was missing. Looking back at him, she thought about how different he was from what she'd originally thought.

"Can we stop here?" she said as she pointed to a bench underneath a large hickory tree that was covered in frost.

"Sure," he said, walking over to the bench and brushing off the white flakes. Lex had never really cared for the cold even though she was born and raised in a cold city. But with Micah, here in Cranberry Heights, everything felt different.

"You're nothing like Evan," she said as they sat on the bench. She didn't really want to bring him up, but she felt inclined to share more about her past since he'd been so open with her.

"When I first met Evan, I was in high school," she said, curling one leg underneath her and turning to her side to face him. "I was on the cheerleading team and he was a football player."

"A cheerleader, huh," he said as his goatee curled to the side at his cunning smirk.

"Yeah, a cheerleader," she said with a laugh. "Back then, it seemed natural for us to be together. You never saw one of us without the other. We were both popular, although I never understood how I'd gotten so popu-

lar. I've always been a little different. A little clumsy…
awkward at times."

"You may be all those things, but that's what's so attractive about you," he chimed in. "Plus, you have a great
personality and you're extremely beautiful, although you
have no idea how striking you are."

Her heart beat faster at his words. She supposed men
had been calling her beautiful her entire life, but every
time she heard Micah say the words, it had a different
effect on her.

"I'll be the first to admit that I need to work on my
insecurities. I know I'm beautiful, intelligent, driven. I
just forget sometimes," she said softly before continuing. "When Evan met me, I had all the confidence in
the world, but somewhere along the line, I lost a part of
that confidence."

"You mean, he made you lose it," he said protectively.

"He definitely played a large part in it. But I let him.
He wanted a trophy wife. Someone who looked good
on his arm and did what he said. And as much as I hate
to admit it, I fell into the role all too easily. I had convinced myself that being with a man like him was what
I wanted."

"What did your family think about him?"

"They couldn't stand him. But while we dated, and
even when we got married, no one had really told me
how much they hated him. But, in their defense, I wasn't
being honest about how controlling he was. They saw
a few signs when we would attend family events, but
whenever they asked me if I was happy, I would lie and
tell them that I was."

"I bet it was hard keeping how you really felt to yourself," Micah said as he began rubbing her knee.

"It was," Lex said, shaking her head. "Especially the brief time we were married. There were many times I thought about telling the girls, but decided against it. Looking back, I realize that I never told anyone anything because I was embarrassed."

"What for?"

"Well, for starters, I was the one who chose to be with a person like that. Guaranteed, he wasn't always like that. But the signs were there in college. We were talking on the phone one day and he heard my roommate's boyfriend in the background and demanded to know who it was. I explained to him who the voice belonged to, but he didn't care. He went to college an hour from where I attended school and he drove down to mine right after our call. That's when his craziness started. We broke up for a while because I couldn't handle how needy he was, and during that time he would leave me messages saying how much he loved me and couldn't live without me. It wasn't the messages themselves that were strange, but rather the amount of calls I received."

"That's insane," Micah said, shaking his head.

"Tell me about it." She shifted in her seat when the brisk wind slashed across her face. "One day, he left me over twenty voice mails."

"Dude clearly had psychological issues," Micah said in irritation. "How did you end up getting back together with him?"

"His parents had moved to New Orleans once Evan went to college and were killed during Hurricane Katrina. He was devastated, and when he told me he couldn't live without me, I felt bad for him and we got back together. We got married right before I graduated, despite my parents' warnings to wait. Almost instantly, Evan started acting crazy again. Screening my calls, placing hidden cameras in our house, watching me while I slept… He claimed he was just protecting me from the dangerous world, but I still didn't feel safe. When I complained about him doing something, he would tell me I was lucky to have him and wasn't that attractive anyway. Then he'd claim I was bad in bed among other things and this was all within our first month of marriage."

"You can't be serious," Micah said as he outstretched her leg over his lap. "I hope you didn't take any of that nonsense to heart."

"At this point, I knew marrying him was a mistake. When I say he broke my confidence and made me more insecure, it wasn't because I believed what he said. It was because I couldn't believe that I had spent so many years of my life with such a jerk. I lost trust in myself and my ability to make the right decision. When Imani, Cyd, Mya and I decided to create Elite Events Incorporated, he found out and had a fit. And then my grandmother, Gamine, passed away, and he starting arguing with me because he felt I was spending so much time with my family. When I got the letter with the story that my grandmother left me, I told him it was over and that all the begging and pleading in the world couldn't convince me to stay. He finally left Chicago and became a financial advisor in New York."

"I'm glad you finally stood up for yourself."

"Me, too," she said with a sigh. "And you know the rest of the story… Him staging the robbery…stealing everything I loved, including my grandmother's brooches."

Micah reached out and gently rubbed his hand on her cheek. She shivered under his soft touch. "Are you ready to head back, superwoman?" he asked with an endearing smile.

"Superwoman? Hardly," she said, standing up from the bench.

"When faced with adversity, you overcame a huge obstacle and re-created yourself into a better person by learning from your experience. Sounds pretty heroic to me."

She looked over at him and reached out for his hand as they began walking. "Thank you for saying that, Micah."

"Anytime," he said, pulling her to him and kissing her forehead.

Chapter 16

Forget falling, Micah thought when they were almost to Madden Manor. *I'm in love with her.* The entire time he listened to her story, one thing became completely evident in his mind. He was going to marry this woman. His mom had always told him and his brothers that when they found the one, they would know. Micah had known that he wanted to date her. He even knew he wanted a committed relationship with her. But now, he knew that neither of the first two options would suffice. She was the one he couldn't live without.

She looked over at him and flashed a smile. He smiled back thinking she had no idea just how much Cranberry Heights would become a part of her life. His mind ventured to the future as he imagined them bringing their kids to Cranberry Heights to stay with his parents. Or Lex's dad, Ethan, telling their kids all his cooking secrets before they could even cook. But he couldn't tell Lex yet. She wasn't ready.

"By the way," Micah said, breaking the silence, "what was the story that your grandmother gave you?"

"I love this story," she said with a grin. "The story was handwritten in a vintage journal about the size of the palm of my hand. It's about a woman who dedicated her entire life to meeting new people in hopes of taking a bit of every person she met to mold herself into the person she wanted to be. In the beginning of the story, the woman has a problem with change and as a result, she has a period in her life when she remains stagnant…not really living to her fullest ability. So for two years, she decides to journey outside of her comfort zone to find herself…to find her purpose by trying new things, visiting new people, eating new foods, learning about different religions. She meets some very impactful people on her journey, including her husband. Each encounter is detailed, along with the quality she chose to remember of that person. After two years, she finally realizes that life is what you make it. Her decisions and the people she met are all a part of her and her story. But she held the power to her life. Not anyone else…"

She leaned her head against Micah's shoulder as they walked.

"The story changed my perspective on life. When I reached the end of the journal, I realized that the narrator of the story was my grandmother and the man she refers to that she met on her journey is my grandfather, Ed Burrstone. The three brooches were a gift from my grandmother's friend, who was born in India and moved to the United States as a teenager with her family. She was the last person she met on her journey. Turns out, the woman was only given a month to live and in her last days, my grandmother happened to volunteer at the senior home where the lady lived. She had conversations with her every day and learned about her life and how she'd never married or had children. She was the last of her United States relatives and she told my grandmother that meeting her had made her last days joyful. A month after the woman passed, my grandmother received a letter from the woman's lawyer stating that the woman had left her three golden brooches that were made in India."

"Wow," Micah exclaimed, wrapping an arm around her shoulders. "That's an amazing story. And it's even more remarkable that your grandmother knew you'd need to hear that story one day."

"Gamine was intuitive that way," Lex said, looking up at Micah. He wiped away a fallen tear from her face.

"Although Imani, Cyd and I haven't discussed it, we each knew that she left us something when she passed. Gamine had a way of communicating with us in a way that our parents couldn't. If I had to guess, I would assume that she left handwritten items for me, Imani and Cyd. We're the three oldest grandchildren and she would always leave us little notes growing up."

When they arrived at the house, they said hello to the guests that were still up before they headed to their own guestroom. "Gamine seems special. I wish I could have met her," Micah said after shutting the bedroom door.

"Me, too," Lex said, placing a soft kiss on his lips before removing her shoes. "But she knows you."

"You think so?" he asked, removing his shoes.

"Yup, because at the end of the story, when she tells me it's about her journey, she also states that one day I will meet someone who will take one look at me and know my self-worth," she said bashfully. "And she said when that happens, I should embrace the feeling…and the person."

As Micah stood there watching emotions cross Lex's face, he was tempted to say the hell with keeping his thoughts to himself and tell her his plan to one day soon make her his. But he was more forthcoming with his feelings and she was just beginning to get accustomed to the idea.

"Thank you for telling me that," he said, crossing the room to her with one goal in mind—getting her out her clothes.

When he reached her, she was already tugging on her shirt, clearly recognizing his intent. He helped her remove her clothes in record speed. Once they had removed her last stitch of clothing, Micah grabbed her arm and walked to the bathroom.

"What about your clothes?" she asked.

"I'll take them off in a minute."

"Why are we in the bathroom?"

Instead of responding to her, Micah plugged the whirlpool tub and began running the hot water.

"Why, Mr. Madden," she said with a devilish smirk, "I think it's only fitting that I tell you that I've never made love in the tub before."

"Then I'm glad I can be your first," he said as he tugged on her ponytail holder to release her hair. Brown waves fell about her shoulders while loose strands teased her cheeks. Pushing the strands out of her face, he thought he'd never seen her look so beautiful. And he was so glad she wasn't hiding her body from him, because if he had his way, she'd never wear another piece of clothing again.

He lifted her onto the marble countertop and brought

his face closer to hers, wondering if she could feel how hard his heart was pounding. She did that to him…made his heart beat uncontrollably just by being near. He'd told her things that he was sure would run some women away, but not Lex. She understood him and, in turn, she trusted him with her own story of her past. Love was never something that he thought was in his future, but he guessed that's what people meant when they said love had a way of sneaking up on you when you least expected it. Lex had come along before he even had a chance to realize what had hit him.

She looked at him with her adorable brown eyes and winked before giggling. Needing to feel her lips, he leaned down and kissed her with all the love he felt.

When a man truly kisses the woman he knows he wants to spend the rest of his life with, that kiss will touch the depths of her soul and build a permanent home right on top of her heart. Mrs. Madden's words echoed in her mind as Lex sat there kissing Micah as if her life depended on it.

To the outside eye, it may appear to be just like any kiss like they'd shared many times before. But internally, Lex's stomach felt like she was riding a never-ending roller coaster. This kiss felt different… He felt different… The air that crackled around them felt different. By now, she knew Micah's lips and how he used them on her. The way he was kissing and suckling her now was definitely not the way he'd kissed her before.

She opened her legs wider and encircled his head with her hands. *What is going on?* she thought, unable to get enough of his taste. Her heartbeat quickened as reality hit her. The emotions in this kiss had surpassed the feelings a man had for a woman he was interested in dating, but instead, embodied the feelings that a man had for a woman he planned on spending the rest of his life with.

He nibbled her lips once more before releasing her lips and resting his forehead on hers. Both of them panted heavily, waiting for oxygen to seep into their lungs. Lex felt like the next minutes moved in slow motion as they struggled to get their breathing under control. Micah lifted his head, his eyes caressing her chin before moving to her lips and nose, settling on her eyes. His penetrating stare made her breathing falter as he gazed into her soul, displaying his emotions for her to interpret as she deemed fit.

In that moment, she fully understood what Mrs. Madden and her grandmother had tried to explain to her. *I fell in love with him*...she thought, her eyes searching his at her internal admission. *I fell,* she thought again. *Hard.* And it wasn't that she fell for him because of attraction or lust. She fell for the man he was in the past, the man he was now and the man he would be in the future. And after a kiss like that, she knew in her heart that Micah Madden wasn't going anywhere...and she loved that feeling.

He glanced over his shoulder at the tub and ran over to turn off the water. "Are you ready to get in?" he asked, testing the water.

"Yes," she said as she slid off the marble top. Even in clothes with his back turned to her, he looked good enough to eat. His hands grasped the bottom of his shirt as he lifted the fabric over his head.

Lex gasped louder than she'd intended at the sight of his full, muscular back. *How did I not notice this before?* she thought as she made her way to him and lightly touched the inked detail permanently splashed across his shoulders. The design of his tattoo made her mouth water to the point that she ran her lips across the edges, not caring if Micah thought she was crazy.

"Be careful," he warned. "I'm letting you do as you please, but if you keep putting your lips on me, I'm turning around to finish the job."

"Okay," she whispered, running her hands over the parts she'd kissed instead. Every woman had a list of qualities that made her weak in the knees. For Lex, muscular arms, nice teeth, a good cook, sexy dimples and tattoos were her top five. The fact that Micah had all five of her drop-your-panties-on-the-spot attributes made it hard for her to stand there without stripping off the rest of his clothes. So she did just that.

"I can't believe I missed this tattoo," she said as she bent down to tug his jeans off.

"The lighting has been really dim when we've been naked," he replied, undoing his belt when he realized what she was doing. "Plus I've kept you occupied in the bedroom so you haven't had a chance to study my body like I have yours."

Well, that's changing tonight, she thought after she got his pants off and went for his boxers. Once his boxers were halfway down his thighs, she let out another squeal. Tattoo number two was located on his left calf and somehow, she'd missed it when she had taken off his pants. Her hands moved to his calf, lightly caressing the design.

"Lex?" Micah's voice interrupted her observation.

"Sorry," she said, removing his boxers and then immediately becoming distracted by his butt. *Tight. Round. Kissable.* Never had Lex wanted to kiss a butt before, but Micah had the type of butt that begged to be kissed. Better yet, it begged to be bitten…so she bit it.

"Um, that's a first," Micah said apprehensively. "Not sure how I feel about you biting my ass."

"I had to," she said as she stood back to view his entire backside. "You are an incredibly tasty-looking man."

"Thanks," he said, glancing over his shoulder. "I'm guessing you have a fascination with tattoos?"

"You have no idea," she said, bringing one hand to her mouth as her eyes continued to roam over him.

"I think I do," he said with a laugh. "I'm turning around now."

Lex should have held on to the towel rack because she hadn't prepared herself for the complete view of his stark naked and very aroused, athletic body. Once again, she'd missed a tattoo on his right arm since she'd been so focused on his back. He also had a tattoo on his left pectoral muscle that flexed under her gaze. She wanted to run her tongue across the ink and pull one of his dark nipples in between her teeth. Her nipples began to harden at the thought. She didn't want to be cliché and bite her fingers to keep from screaming, but she had to. Temptation was too high and the way he was looking at her gave her goose bumps. *The body of a god.* Muscles. Abs. Tats. White teeth. Dimples. Mohawk. Dark eyes.

"Damn," she exhaled aloud as she closed the distance between them.

"You said the *D* word," he said, taunting her. But that wasn't the only curse word floating through her mind at the moment.

"Get in the water," she told him as she pointed to the tub and clicked on the jets.

"Whatever you say, boss," he said with a smirk. "You seem really dominatrix right now."

She was feeling that way, too. But she was tired of

talking. Tired of thinking. And quite frankly, she couldn't think around Micah anyway, with him looking this scrumptious. He sat in the tub with his legs open wide, awaiting her body. She followed him into the tub, immediately getting on her knees the moment her body hit the water. Micah looked at her inquisitively, probably trying to figure out why she was kneeling in front of him. She was nervous to do what her mind was telling her she had to do, so she leaned in to place a seductive kiss on his lips before her hands trailed down his chest and landed on his thighs.

Once at his inner thighs, she twirled her fingers in small circles until she reached the object of her pursuit. She glinted her eyes at him as she wrapped her hand around his shaft and began rotating her hand up and down.

His hands flew to each side of the tub as he slowly let his head fall back in enjoyment. She looked down at the piece in her hand, loving how the tip disappeared when she reached the top. The muffled sounds coming from Micah's mouth were giving her the encouragement she needed to move her hands faster, quicker, making sure she fondled his balls as she did.

"Lex," he blew in a rushed breath as he tilted his head back up to look at her.

"Can you do me a favor?" she asked. Instead of responding he just nodded his head in agreement.

"Scoot up a little so you're on the higher part of the tub."

She really appreciated the different levels that offered seating in the whirlpool tub because she definitely needed him elevated for what she planned to do next. Once he was on the highest level, as she'd predicted, his lower half sprang above the water. She submerged him in her mouth, taking the tip first before pulling him in as deeply as she could.

He jerked at the contact, his eyes widening in awe as she relaxed her throat and deep throated him like she'd never done before.

"Another first," she said in between sucks, wanting him to know she'd never taken another man in her mouth before. Not even her ex-husband.

"For real," he wheezed in a forced voice. She didn't have time to respond. Her mouth was too occupied and her mind was too fascinated by the way he felt sliding in and out of her throat.

"You should stop," he said on the brink. "I'm coming."

Duh, she thought. *That's exactly what I wanted to happen.* So instead of slowing her movements, she went faster, water swishing around them and splashing on the floor. In one sudden spasm, he shuddered irrepressibly, giving Lex the pleasure of knowing she'd been the cause of his satisfaction.

Chapter 17

"Shh," Micah said to Lex as they hid behind a large pine tree in the park, trying not to move as they heard the sound of snow crunching around them. From the anxious look on her face, he could tell that Lex had really enjoyed the different Snowlympics' contests.

Micah felt like a new man after such an exhilarating night with Lex. They'd gotten more snow overnight, making for a perfect day of winter festivities. The morning had begun with the sledding competition that required teams to sled down the biggest hill in town six times. The fastest ten teams moved on to the next round. Lex had been great at that, developing a technique that caused her to fly down the hill past other contestants. Next, there was a snow-ice-cream eating challenge in which one of two team members had to finish an entire oversize bowl of ice cream made of snow. The top seven teams moved on to the next round and Micah had nailed it and finished in second place.

After that, teams competed to see who could build the most unique snowman and Lex had the idea to build a beach snowman laying in a reclining lawn chair wearing sunglasses, a large summer hat, a bikini and holding a beer in one twigged hand. The judges had loved their idea, landing them one of five spots in the final round… a snowball fight.

But this wasn't just any snowball fight. Each team had a safe zone where they could reload on snowballs but other teams couldn't hit them while there. Each snowball had a paintball inside, five colors for five teams, and both team members had to remain within the war zone or else that team would be eliminated. When they had originally begun putting on their winter snowball-fight gear, Lex had looked hesitant after sizing up the other groups competing.

"Are you ready?" he asked her quietly, making sure her helmet was secure before they left the tree they were hiding behind.

"I think so," she said, taking a lipstick tube out her pocket to reapply a fresh pink coat.

"Are you serious right now," Micah said in disbelief. "We're in the middle of war and you're putting on lipstick."

"I'm nervous," she said in a frustrated whisper as she rubbed the color across her lips. "Leave me alone."

Her mouth opened and parted to make sure it was applied perfectly. The gesture reminded Micah of where her mouth had been placed the night before and how she'd used it to seduce him into submission. He looked down at his pants. *Great…a hard-on in the middle of a war zone.*

She then pulled out another tube of clear gloss to apply to her lips on top of the color.

"I wouldn't put on that lip gloss if I were you," he said firmly. "Unless you want me to take you on this tree and say to hell with winning."

Her eyes grew big in surprise at his comment, but she ignored his warning and began applying the gloss extra slowly. *Fine, have it your way,* he thought, inching toward her. The move caught her off guard and she fumbled with her lip gloss, which eventually fell into the snow.

"Shiitake mushrooms," Micah said, beating Lex to the punch while snapping his fingers for affect.

Lex shot him a harsh stare. "You must think you're so cute," she said with irritation before bending down to try and find her lip gloss.

Micah returned to the game as she searched. "We have to move from this tree," he said after she'd located her lip gloss. She nodded her head and followed his movements as they left behind the large tree. From what he could tell, two other teams were still in this. He motioned for Lex to go left, while he went right. She obeyed and they went in opposite directions. Unlike some competitions, if one team member was out, the other could still participate and take the win. So even if Lex got taken out, he planned on winning Snowlympics.

He crept behind another tree and counted to three before he nailed an opposing team member. Moving with ease through the trees, he reached the partner, eliminating a complete team. *Only one team left,* he thought, creeping behind a large bush. Out of the corner of his eye, he saw movement and noticed it was Lex. *Damn!* What was she doing out in the open? He waved one arm to try and get her attention. No use.

Micah eased from behind the bush just in time to see an opposing member headed toward her with a snowball. Moving swiftly, he tossed his snowball toward the individual, making contact on his shoulder, getting him out.

"Lex, let's go," Micah yelled as he was almost near her. Suddenly, a snowball whipped in his direction, hitting him right in the chest.

"Son of a—" his voice trailed upon realization that he was out of the competition. Even worse, he'd lost sight of Lex. He wanted to try and find her, but a referee was already directing him to leave the war zone. As he was walking from the area, his steps faltered when he heard screams that he knew belonged to Lex even though he couldn't see her. "Damn," he grumbled aloud. Micah hated losing, and the only thing that irritated him more than losing was coming in second place.

"I'm so proud of you," Micah told her for the fifth time since she'd come running from the war zone screaming in joy. Lex couldn't believe that she had won the snowball fight after being scared out her mind most of the duration of the snowball fight. Once she'd seen Micah get hit, she knew there was only one other person in the competition along with her. And since the other person was a high school football player, the odds were against her.

Once the football player had finally cornered her, she'd done the only thing she could think about doing in an uncomfortable situation...run like crazy. But he'd been right on her tail and just when he'd chucked his snowball in her direction, she'd tripped over a large branch that had been buried in the snow. Thinking as quickly as she could on the ground, she turned on her back and swung her snowball in his direction and hit him right in the leg. When the ref announced that the football player was out, Lex had jumped off the ground and screamed at the top of her lungs in excitement.

Now they were in Madden Manor enjoying the Christmas party with all the guests at the B and B, who were discussing how great the winter festival was and congratulating her and Micah on winning Snowlympics. Dessert was being served soon, but Lex had gotten a text from Cyd asking if she and Micah could call them.

"Is this regarding more wedding plans?" Micah asked Lex when they arrived at the bedroom.

"Cyd didn't say, but I think so," she said as she dialed Cyd's number. Cyd picked up on the third ring.

"Hey, guys," Cyd said cheerfully. "Just so you know, the whole gang is together right now and we have you on speakerphone."

After Lex and Micah exchanged hellos to the group, it was Imani who spoke next.

"Well, I know Cyd may have sent out the text to get you all here, but the news we wanted to share is actually about Daman and I." The other line grew silent. "We're having a baby," Imani and Daman said in unison. "We wanted to wait until after the first trimester before we said anything," Imani continued.

"Ahhhh," Lex screamed in the phone as she jumped up and down. "We're so happy for you guys."

"Congrats," Micah added after Lex. Imani and Daman thanked them both before Cyd got back on the phone.

"I wanted to make sure you heard the news," Cyd said. "I suspected that's what they had to share because I caught Daman swapping out the liquor in Imani's cup for apple juice during the Friends-giving drinking game. And my parents have been way too happy lately."

Lex laughed into the phone. "I bet! Thanks for calling, Cyd. We'll see you all soon."

"Wow," Lex said, looking to Micah after ending the call. "The first baby in our generation. I can't wait to spoil him or her."

Her thoughts wandered as she imagined her and Micah walking down Lake Michigan in Chicago with her belly as big as a watermelon.

"What are you thinking about?" Micah asked.

"Nothing," she said, pulling him by his arm. "Let's rejoin the party."

Once they reached the living room, Lex spotted a cozy seat right in front of the fireplace.

"Hey, Dad," Micah said when Mr. Madden walked past them, just as Lex and Micah were sitting down. "Can I talk to you for a second?"

Mr. Madden stopped in his tracks and looked at his son in surprise. Lex glanced over at Mrs. Madden just in time to see her clutch her hand to her heart.

"Sure, son," Mr. Madden finally said before the two walked into the kitchen.

Lex desperately wished she were a fly on the wall for their conversation. Micah had promised her he would have a conversation with his father before they went back to Chicago, but she hadn't known when.

Mrs. Madden glanced over at Lex and angled her head toward the door as she stood from her seat and walked toward the kitchen. Mrs. Madden gently cracked the door so that her husband and son wouldn't hear it creak.

"How do they sound?" Lex whispered when she reached Mrs. Madden.

Mrs. Madden smiled as she let the door softly close. "There voices don't sound tense like they usually do when they talk. I don't know what you said to my son, but my husband has been waiting years to have this conversation."

Lex just smiled as she linked arms with Mrs. Madden and they returned to the guests who were diving into another lip-smacking holiday pie.

"Let me start by saying that I am truly sorry for everything I put you through when I was younger," Micah said, taking a seat opposite his dad.

At his dad's silence, he continued. "I never thought about how my actions would affect you and Mom and at the time. It was hard for me to discontinue relationships that I had in Little Rock."

Mason creased an eyebrow before responding. "I wasn't disappointed in the fact that you maintained unhealthy relationships with men I felt you should ignore. It was more the fact that you let that nonsense follow you to college. I never wanted any of my sons to go down the same path that I went down."

"But dad, sometimes you have to learn lessons the hard way."

"I know that," Mason interjected, "but no matter what I said to you, you never seemed to listen."

"You were a great father. But not once did we have a conversation about your past and the things you went through growing up in Little Rock."

Mason shook his head. "That's because I knew you were my spontaneous son. The one who would push his limit just like I did. I didn't want to give you any ideas."

"Letting me know that you understood what I was going through at the time would have worked better than pushing me off for Mom and Uncle Barry to deal with."

"You only listened to the two of them, Micah. You never listened to what I told you."

"Only because I didn't know you were speaking from experience. It always came across as judgment and disappointment that I couldn't be more like Malik."

Mason squinted his eyes before clasping his hands together on the table. "I never wanted you to be more like Malik or any of your brothers and I'm sorry if I didn't make that clear. What I should have told you back then was that I knew that out of all my sons, you were a force to be reckoned with. All my sons are amazing men, but you had that extra something... You still do. I've always been proud of you, and now that you've started your security company with Shawn, you seem to have truly found your purpose, I couldn't be prouder."

Micah let out a breath he hadn't known he'd been holding as he stared at a man he felt like he was meeting for the first time. *He's proud of me.* He'd heard his dad tell his brothers that, but the words had never been directed at him. A man and his pride was something Micah knew all too well, and it seemed his dad had written the book on it. He leaned back in his chair and dragged his fingers over his face.

"To think of all the years we wasted avoiding this conversation," Micah said, annoyed at himself for not telling his dad how he felt sooner. And frustrated at his dad for never understanding that of all the people in his life, he was the one person he needed approval from. Finally having that approval was slowly filling a void he had in his heart.

"Hold on to Lex," his dad said, breaking his thoughts.

"That came out of nowhere," Micah said with a laugh. Mason joined in the laughter before his face grew serious.

"You and I are a lot alike, and men like us could search our entire lives to find a woman who truly understands us. When I found your mother, I honestly had no idea what she saw in me, but through her love, I was able to find my way and truly become a man. She saw in me what I was trying to see in myself and she didn't care that I didn't have a penny to my name or that our dinner the first few months of our marriage consisted of canned beans and bread. She loved me anyway because she saw the man I was growing to be. She knew we had all this in our future," he added, waving his hands around. "You found your path in life a lot quicker than I did, Micah, but that doesn't mean you don't need a woman who gets you now, accepts where you came from and sees where you're headed in the future."

"I agree," Micah said as he looked at his dad through a new set of eyes. "I haven't told her how I feel yet, but I plan to tell her soon. Even though she's her own woman, the way she understands me reminds me so much of Mom." Micah studied the worry lines permanently etched on his dad's face. Mason was still a healthy and handsome man, but in that moment, Micah realized how much time they'd lost on nonsense.

"So," Micah said, smiling at his dad in a way he couldn't remember smiling in years, "according to mom, you were a troublemaker back in the day. What did you do?"

Mason laughed and shook his head. "What didn't I do," he said as he proceeded to tell Micah stories about the antics he had caused when he was younger.

Chapter 18

Lex looked around her apartment for the tenth time trying to make sure everything was perfect. Although she'd shared many nights with Micah in Cranberry Heights, it was their fourth night being together in Chicago, but the first night they were having dinner at her place instead of his.

She grinned as she lit scented candles throughout her home and thought about the way Micah had acted when they had arrived back in Chicago. The plane had barely landed before he was hightailing it out of O'Hare airport, grabbing their bags and telling the cab to go directly to his condo. They had agreed on a committed relationship before they had left Arkansas, although Micah had admitted he hadn't dated or had sex with anyone since he met her in the lingerie boutique. Lex hadn't either, concluding that they had been acting like an exclusive couple anyway.

She heard a firm knock on the door and checked her clock. *Right on time.* Giving herself another once-over in the mirror, she smoothed out her navy blue cotton dress, fluffed her curls and reapplied a quick coat of Burberry lipstick. She briefly contemplated sliding on some slippers, but she opted to show off her freshly pedicured toes.

The moment she opened the door, her breath caught and her lips parted. When he'd asked her how he should dress, she'd told him to dress comfortably, and she figured she would surprise him and wear a cute dress in hopes of catching him off guard. Standing in the doorway with him in his heather-gray jogging outfit, white tee, basketball shoes and baseball cap, she was the one who was caught off guard by how sexy he looked. She couldn't recall ever seeing him look this casual and it was causing her insides to twist and turn wildly.

"Are you going to invite me in?" Micah asked.

"Sorry," she said, stepping aside. The minute she shut the door, Micah pulled her to him for an explosive kiss, giving her a chance to get reacquainted with his addicting taste. His mouth consumed hers in such an erotic way; she felt it all the way to the tips of her toes. She moaned into his mouth when his hands found their way to her behind and gripped her dress, sliding the material up past her waist.

When his palms met her flesh, she opened her eyes just in time to catch the inquisitive look in his eyes. He lifted her dress even more and glanced over her shoulder to her butt.

"You must not want us to eat dinner," he said upon realizing she wasn't wearing any panties.

"You weren't supposed to figure that part out yet," she

said, gently pulling the back of her dress down. "Come on. I'll give you a tour."

She led him through her condo and informed him that she wasn't showing him her bedroom until after dinner. Luckily, he didn't put up much of a fuss.

"What's for dinner?" he asked when they'd arrived at the dining room table.

"I'm so glad you asked," she said as she motioned for him to take a seat. "As you can see, we have a fresh salad and dinner rolls."

"Both look great."

"Thank you! And for the main entrée, we have green beans that I personally picked from my dad's garden and…" Her voice trailed off as she rounded the table to lift the cover that was concealing the main dish. "We have filet mignon and lobster tail with my special butter, garlic and herb sauce."

"Damn, girl," Micah exclaimed, looking over the entire spread. "I didn't know you were throwing down dinner like this."

"Told ya I'm good," she said with a laugh. "I also have a red wine that goes great with the filet mignon."

"I must admit," he said, shaking his head, "I was all set to take you to your bedroom first and eat dinner after, but this looks too good to ignore right now."

"Then let's eat," she said, pouring him a glass of wine and taking a seat across from him. "Besides, you'll need to keep up your strength for what I have planned later."

He didn't say anything, but the intense way he watched her told her all she needed to know. He was ready for whatever she had in store.

An hour and a half later, they'd finished dinner and washed the dishes. Micah was placing the packaged left-

overs in the refrigerator and Lex knew this was her time
to set the mood.

"Micah, when you finish, can you meet me in the living room?"

"Sure," he said, glancing at her with excitement in
his eyes.

After he agreed, Lex went into the living room and
dimmed the lighting before turning on her electric fireplace. All the candles that were burning in the living
room and bedroom were a jasmine and lavender mix—
scents that were proven to heighten a man's desires.

She glanced around the room making sure nothing
would get in the way of what she had planned next. She
didn't hear Micah come into the room, but her nipples
hardened the minute the stimulating scent of musk and
man oozed into her nostrils, taking over her senses. She
found comfort in knowing she didn't have to see him to
know he was in close proximity to her.

"I'll be right back," she said, discreetly grabbing the
remote to the iPod docking station. She pointed to the
couch, indicating for him to sit before leaving the room.
Once she was in the confines of her bedroom with the
door locked, she walked over to her iPhone and popped
in her headphones before scrolling through her audio-
books and pressing play.

"Congratulations on completing your journey to self-
discovery," the voice said through her headphones. "Now
that you have realized your self-worth, you can conquer
anything you want in life. Maybe take a chance on a new
relationship with that special person you've had your
eye on."

As the voice spoke to her, Lex stepped out of her dress
and dabbed some jasmine and lavender body oil on the in-

timate parts of her body before changing into something she was sure would bring Micah to his knees.

"Show that person that you can take charge and be the aggressor."

Lex added silver glitter pumps to her sexy outfit before running her fingers through her hair and throwing some gloss on her lips.

"Okay," she said, standing in front of her full-length mirror before she resumed listening to her audiobook. "The time is now! Don't keep your future waiting."

Lex cut off the audiobook and tossed her phone in a drawer before retuning to the mirror. "Tonight, you aren't Lex Turner, the woman who plays it safe," she said firmly. "Tonight, you're a woman whose ultimate goal is to seduce the man you fell in love with and prove that you're not the shy girl he met months ago." She really didn't need a pep talk, but she gave herself one anyway. She'd already stepped outside her comfort zone with Micah and she felt like she was gaining back the confidence that she'd lost after her relationship with Evan.

She stepped out into the hallway and angled her hand so that she could click on the music without Micah seeing her. The minute she heard Beyoncé's latest hit, she had immediately made a mental note to keep the song in the back of her mind. She'd been practicing her striptease all day, and now she was ready for Micah to see what loving him was doing to her.

Micah glanced around when the music suddenly came through the speakers. He didn't see Lex, but the hairs on the back of his neck stood on alert. He removed his jacket, too overcome with heat to sit on the couch fully clothed.

As soon as Beyoncé's voice started singing, Lex's leg

appeared from the side of the wall. Long. Sexy. Enclosed in a sexy silver heel. Micah leaned up in his seat, anticipating what would happen next.

When she turned the corner, his breath caught when he realized she was wearing the pleated lilac babydoll and silky lace boyshort that she'd purchased at Bare Sophistication lingerie boutique. *Oh, my damn,* he thought when he realized the scene that was unfolding in front of him. *A striptease...in my outfit no less.* He knew it wasn't really his outfit, but it felt like it was. Since the moment he'd rung it up for her, he'd wished he could see it on her.

Deciding he needed to enjoy this moment, he leaned back on the sofa and linked his hands behind his head. When she finally stood completely in front of him, he realized she was singing along to the song and her voice was amazing. She even harmonized, going low when Beyoncé sang high and vice versa.

She danced in front of him dipping her butt just to bring it back again and tossing her legs around as if she danced professionally every day. When she walked to the wall and did a quick in and out hip movement, he almost lost it finding it hard to enjoy the dance in it's entirety when he was hung up on the way her fingers slid down the wall and her back curved to make her butt pop out more.

After a couple minutes, she began making her way to the sofa. *Oh, shit,* he thought when she stopped within inches of his grasp, turned her back to him and eased all the way down to the floor before bringing herself back up. When she bent over, giving him an exposed view of her behind covered in the racy lace material, he lost it. His hands gripped her before she had a chance to turn around.

"Micah," she said with a giggle as she glanced over her shoulder. "I'm not finished yet."

"Oh, you're done," he said, standing up and throwing her over his shoulders. She yelped at the sudden overtaking.

He scanned the rooms until he located her bedroom and tossed her on the bed. "You couldn't honestly think I could make it through that entire dance without touching you, did you?"

Instead of answering him, she flashed him a look of innocence, but there was nothing innocent about that dance she'd just given him. He could hear another slow song starting to play and although the sound was faint, he decided to leave the bedroom door open so that they could make love to the music.

"I've been thinking about seeing you in this lingerie outfit since you bought it," he said as he watched her play with the edges of the babydoll. He took a mental picture, wanting to always remember how free and uninhibited she looked in this moment. Unable to hold back any longer, he quickly removed all his clothes and covered himself before joining her on the bed kissing every part of her body that wasn't hidden underneath material.

"Aren't you going to take off my heels and clothes?" she asked.

"Hell, no," he said loudly. "I'm making love to you in this babydoll with those sexy shoes on. And," he said as his fingers went in between her thighs, "since these panties have a slit in the center, we're definitely keeping these on."

He began massaging her clit with his fingers, gradually dipping in two fingers when he felt her getting hotter and wetter.

"Micah," she breathed as she began rotating her hips to the movement of his hand. When he felt her on the edge, he increased the pace of his fingers until his hand was soaking wet from her juices.

Her eyes grew dark and her breathing became labored...signs of a strong orgasm. He opened her legs and eased himself inside of her, loving the fact that he could make love to her at the same time he admired her in her underwear.

Her sweet moans filled the room and were quickly joined by his intense groans. She felt so good. Too good. He wanted to make this last for as long as he could, but sexing her in lingerie was becoming a new fetish of his and the fact that she looked so damn sexy was making it harder for him to refrain from coming.

"I want to flip on all fours," she said between pumps. *All fours? Ah, hell...* There was no way he could last long if she wanted him to hit it from the back.

He obliged her request and re-entered her from the back, the lacy material floating about her body with each thrust of his hips. She met him pump for pump, rotating her hips as she did so. Through pure miracle, he managed to push aside his growing need to release his juices and was able to add two additional sexual positions to their sensual rendezvous.

"I'm coming," she said in the sexiest voice he'd ever heard from her. Her words were music to his ears, since he was once again on the brink of exploding. With two more thrusts, they both released orgasms so powerful that they succumbed to fatigue.

"Wow," Micah said, heaving on the bed with Lex right by his side.

"Tell me about it," she said, leaning up to lightly kiss

him. They locked eyes and kissed once more with more hunger and potency than their prior kiss.

"I want to tell you something," he said after a few moments of silence. Lex gazed up to him, waiting to hear what he had to say.

"I love you," he stated as he watched her eyes fill with emotion.

"I love you, too," she said with a smile as she scooted closer to him.

She loves me, he thought as he smiled back and kissed her hard.

He loves me, she thought as she sat near her bay window drinking a much-needed cup of coffee. After their admission last night, they'd made love several more times before falling asleep. Micah had awakened her after only three hours of sleep for a quickie, and to let her know he had to run home to change for a meeting, promising to be back soon.

She already couldn't wait for him to hurry back. She was in her prime and was finally living her life, not dwelling on bad decisions she'd made in the past that had led to her biggest failed relationship. *Maybe I had to go through that to find and appreciate a man like Micah.*

When she heard the knock on her door, she secured her robe, although she briefly considered answering the door for Micah naked. She couldn't wait to tell him about all her revelations since they hadn't gotten a chance to talk last night after her striptease.

She swung open the door. "Hello, sweetheart," said a repulsive voice that had only appeared in her nightmares. *Please tell me I'm still sleeping.*

She'd often heard people say that you can't outrun

your past. As she stood there staring at the person on the other side of her door, it seemed the past she'd been running from and trying to forget had just popped up on her doorstep.

Chapter 19

"What are you doing here and how did you get past security?" she asked the man, demanding an answer. "And you're supposed to be in New York."

"I can't come visit my hometown and see my wife," Evan Gilmore said with a devious smile.

"Ex-wife," she replied quickly.

"Details, details," he said, trying to push his way through the door. "Security was busy so I decided to let myself up."

"I didn't invite you in," she said, pushing him back through the door. "And I'm calling security to escort you back out."

"Speaking of security, you may want to hear what I have to say before you kick me out," Evan said firmly.

"I'm not interested in anything you have to say."

"Even if it's about your little boy toy, Micah Madden?" Evan said, succeeding in getting her interest.

"He's none of your concern."

"He is when he puts the woman I used to love in danger."

"Love? Is that what you tell yourself every night?" Lex said, her voice getting higher.

"I did love you," Evan argued. "Besides, I may have been a lot of things, but I never forced myself on another woman."

"Excuse me," Lex said in irritation. "I don't know what the hell you're talking about and I need you to leave." She started to close the door on him.

"At least look at this file," Evan said, stopping the door with his arm. "Micah isn't the man you think he is. I don't have to come in, but at least meet with me before I go back to New York. After being together for so long you at least owe me that."

Lex opened the door back up. "Let's get one thing straight. I don't owe you one damn second of my time, nor do I care what you're up to. Once I shut this door on you, I plan to forget that your sorry ass ever existed, and I suggest you stay away from me unless you want me to get a restraining order."

Evan laughed maliciously and started clapping his hands together. "Bravo, Lex, bravo. Seems you gave up that stupid no-cursing rule."

"I only curse when I need to, and when it comes to scum like you, I have to stoop to your level to get my point across."

"Oh, I see," Evan said, leaning against the doorjamb. "You must think this guy Micah actually loves you and wants to be with you. I heard about him and trust me, you aren't the type of woman he's into. You're the girl next door…the nice girl…the *basic* girl. When he's done playing it safe with you he'll go back to the type of women he prefers dating. The kind of independent and feisty woman you'll never be."

"Go to hell," she said, balling her hand in a fist to refrain from slapping him.

"Already headed there," he said, holding the file out again. "And it seems your boy will be joining me there." He tossed the file through the door onto the floor.

"Read the file," Evan said. "Because if I have my way, I'll tell the press who the true Micah Madden is and dash any hopes of him really getting that stupid security company off the ground. And what's the name of their biggest recent investor? Grant & Parker Inc. is it? Did I forget to mention that I'm the financial advisor for Ben Grant and Liam Parker? Oh, yeah, I have clients all over the United States, not just Chicago and New York. Imagine my surprise when I was on a conference call with them and they mentioned having a great dinner with a new company they are investing in. What a shame that Shawn Miles will go down because he partnered with a shady guy like Madden."

"I've heard enough," Lex said as she shut the door again. "Don't ever come here again."

"I won't have to," he said behind the slammed door. "After you read what's in the file you'll be calling me."

She looked through her peephole to make sure he was gone. Usually she always checked the peephole before answering the door, but her mind had been elsewhere.

"He's gone," she said to herself as she tried to slow her heartbeat. She hadn't seen him in over six years and she'd hoped she went the rest of her life without seeing him again. As she got up from the door, she glanced at the file before picking it up off the floor and going to her desk.

Once she was seated, she opened the file and began reading the contents inside. She didn't really know what she was looking for until she got to a document from Fisk University. Micah's freshman year transcript was included. *He is smart,* she thought, taking note of all the A's and B's. During his first year, he'd even joined a business fraternity on campus that was really hard for freshman students to enter.

Lex was still wearing a smile when she got to one of two police reports, one from the campus police and one from the Nashville, Tennessee, police. Her smile dropped instantly.

"What the…" She scanned both documents, reading a detailed account about Micah's arrest in college. One of the statements in the report momentarily stopped her breathing.

"Micah Madden and Neil Timmons took turns sexually assaulting me against my will," Lex read aloud, quoted from a woman named Ashley Anderson. Lex sat there and read both police reports from top to bottom before looking at the final document that was a picture of Ashley after the attack. The image made Lex drop the entire file out of her hands.

One hand flew to her mouth and she leaned back in her desk chair. She couldn't believe what she was reading, and as she recalled all the details of her conversations with Micah, she remembered that he never told her what he had been arrested for.

The case was dropped based off of false evidence… His words swirled around in her mind. As she sat there, recounting everything that Micah had ever told her, she knew what was in the file couldn't be true. But still, there was a little voice inside her head that wondered how big of a role he actually played. She was aggravated that he hadn't come right out and told her what had happened.

She ran and got her work cell phone, which would allow her number to appear unknown to whomever she called, and dialed Evan's number. He answered on the second ring.

"These accusations are false," she said as soon as he answered.

"You're smarter than you look," Evan stated. "Even so, the info is still out there. If I have a friend who was able to dig it up, so are many others."

"What's your point, Evan?" she yelled. "Micah was cleared of all charges so whatever you're thinking about doing would be pointless."

"Think again, sweetheart," he said in a tone that made her want to throw up. "You met Ben Grant's wife at dinner, right? Denise Grant?"

"Yes, and…?"

"Did you know they have a daughter named Monica Grant?"

"They mentioned that's their only daughter. What's your point?"

"My point, Lex, is that dear sweet Monica didn't have the best experience at Arkansas State University. You see, Monica had an off-campus job and decided to help out a friend and take an overnight shift. She should have returned to campus before it got dark because she was waiting for the bus when she was sexually assaulted by a man who dragged her away from the bus and into an alley where there were more men waiting to sexually assault her. The entire ordeal was so devastating that Monica never fully recovered, and although the men were brought to justice, it wasn't enough to make Monica feel safe again."

"That is heart-wrenching" Lex exclaimed as she wiped a tear from her eye and placed her hand over her heart. "My heart aches for them, but I'm still not understanding. I met them and there is no way Ben and Denise Grant would hold it against Micah that he was falsely accused of something he didn't do."

"You may be right," Evan responded. "But they would if they knew Micah used to hang out in the same crowd as Neil Timmons, Monica's main attacker."

Oh, goodness, no... She tried to comprehend what Evan was telling her, but one thing still wasn't adding up. "Why are you involving yourself in this? What do you want?"

"Isn't it obvious," he said deceitfully. "The only thing that will stop me from informing Ben and Denise Grant about Micah is you. I want you back Lex. I want you back and I want us to get remarried."

Blackmail. Lex dropped the phone, refusing to listen to anything else Evan had to say. She went to the couch and lay down before she picked up her personal cell and told Micah she wasn't feeling well and needed some time to herself.

She knew he didn't deserve to be ignored and quite frankly, all she wanted to do was tell him everything she'd just found out. But a part of her didn't understand how Micah could be friends with a man like Neil Timmons. An even larger part was worried that Evan's accusations were true. Lex wasn't the type of woman Micah usually dated. *Could he have pursued me because he thought I was easily influenced?* She rubbed her forehead. *How much do I actually know about Micah?*

Guaranteed, she'd spent the past few weeks getting to know him and his family, so her heart was telling her to trust her gut and believe that there was nothing Micah would have in common with a man like Neil. Micah loved her...the real her. Unlike Evan, he didn't have any ulterior motives in dating her.

Lex stood and began pacing the floor. She'd been wrong in the past. Evan was proof of that. Even so, Evan Gilmore had ruined her life years ago, and she'd promised when she divorced him that she would never give him that power again. Micah was finally in a place that he wanted to be in with the type of job he'd always dreamed of having.

As soon as she figured out how to make Evan back off without getting Micah involved, she would talk to Micah about the entire situation and handle her relationship without Evan's interference. Until then, she would not do anything to jeopardize the rise of M&M Security.

"Hey, Malik," Micah said when his brother, who was also a private investigator, walked into the conference room at M&M Security. When his brother had asked to meet with him and Shawn, Micah knew it had to be important if he was driving from Detroit to Chicago.

He wanted to know what was up with his brother, but right now, he wanted to know what was going on with Lex more. He had no idea what was bothering her and she hadn't returned any of his calls in three days, only text messages. With Christmas approaching in two days he had hoped they would have made plans to spend the holiday together. *She probably got cold feet after I told her I loved her.* But she said she loved him, too, so he didn't understand the problem.

"Micah, are you listening," Malik said, interrupting his thoughts.

"Sorry, bro, what's up?"

"We have a problem," Malik said as he placed his black bag on the mahogany conference table before removing his black winter coat and taking a seat near Shawn and Micah.

"You know how I often run a background check on you to make sure there are no red flags?"

"I thought you ran a background check on me to make sure I wasn't doing something I shouldn't be doing," Micah replied with a sarcastic laugh.

"I'm being serious," Malik said as he took a couple pieces of paper out of his bag and slid them over to Shawn and Micah.

"It looks like somebody on the inside released information on your case from college," Malik said to Micah. "From what I can tell, the hacking took place in the New York City FBI office. Upon further digging, I uncovered the name Ralph Peters as the FBI agent who was investigating you."

"I've never heard of him," Micah said, shuffling through the papers.

"Neither have I," Shawn added.

"I hadn't either so I investigated some more and looked into the people he was associated with. For the most part, the people he hangs out with are clean. But one name stood out."

Malik slipped another paper on the table. "Evan Gilmore is his financial advisor, and according to the background check I did, he was married to—"

"Lexus Turner," Micah interrupted, having permanently etched the name in his mind the minute Lex had told him about Evan. "If he thinks he can get to me to get to Lex, he better think again," he continued, taking a swig from his water bottle to calm his nerves.

"I don't think that's all," Malik added. "Gilmore is the financial advisor for Grant & Parker Incorporated."

"Shit," Micah voiced. "Gilmore handles their finances. So this is more about bringing me down than getting back at Lex."

"I think it's about both," Malik said. "There were quite a few complaints filed against Gilmore from old clients who said he was manipulative, irresponsible and a snake in the grass. Most of the cases were dropped."

"Did you uncover why?" Shawn asked. "I can't imagine most of the cases being dropped when money is involved."

"You're exactly right," Malik stated as he pulled out yet another file that contained a list of names. "Gentlemen, if you look at the first page you will notice all the names of the accounts that Gilmore embezzled money from, and if you look at the second page of names you will find all of the people who he is currently working with or paid off for silence."

"This asshole," Micah stated, pushing all the paper away from him in frustration.

"I also found out that he's in Chicago right now," Malik added. "He's been here for about three days."

"That's right around the time Lex stopped talking to me. I wonder if he contacted her."

"Did you tell her about Fisk University?" Malik asked.

"She knows the story about my past and the trouble I used to get into. And she knows I was arrested and had to transfer schools, but she doesn't know the entire story about Ashley Anderson's accusations."

"If he contacted her, that explains why she hasn't spoken to you," Shawn said. "He could have told her the entire story and she could have been caught off guard because she didn't know."

"Maybe," Micah said, clasping his hands together on the table. "Okay, so what does Grant & Parker Inc. have to do with all this? They aren't on either of Gilmore's list."

Malik opened his mouth to speak and then hesitated.

"What is it?" Micah asked.

"Well," Malik said as he flipped through a couple pages of the file in his hand before slipping it to Micah, "if you read that, you'll see a detailed description of what happened to Ben and Denise Grant's daughter, Monica Grant."

Micah began reading the police report and the statement from Monica, growing angrier with every sentence he read about the sexual assault. No woman should ever have to go through what she went through, and no parent should ever have to watch his or her daughter go through that. It was amazing that she survived the ordeal, but the physical and mental damage that was done was just as devastating to read. Micah had done a good job at keeping his anger under control until he got to the last sentence of the report. *Sexual Offender—Neil Timmons.*

"Damn," Micah yelled as he threw the paper across the table and firmly hit the desk before he stood up to stand by the window.

"Oh, man," he heard Shawn say aloud after reading the document.

"I get it," Micah said, turning from the window to face Malik and Shawn. "Gilmore plans to tell Ben and Denise Grant that I used to hang out in the same circle as Timmons. Am I right? A sure way for M&M Security to lose our biggest investor yet."

"That's my guess," Malik said, walking to Micah and clasping a hand on his shoulder. "But you never know what could happen. I think a better question would be what bug did Evan Gilmore place in Lex's ear. You couldn't have known that Neil would turn out to be the type of man he did. We knew he was bad news, but most the guys in the neighborhood were into the same stuff he was, only he turned into a sexual offender. Plus, I'm sure Grant & Parker would be interested to learn this information about their financial advisor. We need to figure out what we're going to do next."

"I have to talk to Lex," Micah said. "You can work out a plan with Shawn while I'm gone. But first, I think I need to talk to Evan Gilmore."

"That's not a good idea," Shawn said. "I think we should both go."

"I'm going, too," Malik added, packing up his papers. "I figured you would want to talk to him after we uncovered this information, so I found out what hotel he's staying at."

"Great, let's go."

Chapter 20

"Let's sit over there," Lex said to Mya as they made their way to the corner of the sandwich shop attached to the hotel where Evan had asked her to meet him. After days of avoiding Micah and trying to keep everything that was happening to herself, she had finally decided that she needed to open up and talk to someone. She'd debriefed Mya on the situation and asked her to accompany her to the meeting with Evan. After spending thirty minutes trying to convince her to call Micah and ignore Evan's warning altogether, Mya had finally caved in and decided to come with her.

"This is a bad idea," Mya said as they sat at the table.

"Relax," Lex said as she removed her coat and draped it over the back of the chair. "I refuse to give Evan any power over me and I do plan on talking to Micah about this, but only after I give Evan a piece of my mind."

"Look, honey," Mya said, rubbing her hand, "I love this new fierce and fabulous you, but Evan isn't worth the air you breathe. He's lower than the scum on the bottom of your pumps. He's a jerk. He's a scummy jerk. He's a scummy, manipulating, evil, malicious jerk who should pay for the crap he put you through. My only hope is that when Micah finds out, Evan will curse the day he ever coerced you into saying I do."

Lex looked at her partner who was also one of her best friends. "Are you done?"

"Um, yeah, I think so," Mya said, taking a sip from the glass of water that had been brought to the table.

"Do you feel better now?" Lex asked.

"I do," Mya said, giving a quick smile. "But he better not say anything stupid because if he does, I may stab him with my fork."

Lex laughed although nothing about the situation was funny. Mya had always been her ride-or-die friend and she loved that about her. Many people knew that Mya's words were lethal. If she loved you, then you would always have a fierce and loyal friend in Mya, but if you crossed her, or someone she loved, Mya was a force to be reckoned with.

"Oh, great," Mya said, glancing into the lobby of the hotel. "There goes that son-of-a-bitch now."

"Mya," Lex exclaimed. "Can we try to refrain from all the name-calling when he actually gets here? Anger won't resolve this. I need to be able to vocalize what I'm feeling once and for all."

Mya was about to say something else, when Lex cut her off.

"Is that Shawn?" Lex asked when she noticed Evan had stopped walking.

"Uh, I think so," Mya said, peering out of the restaurant.

"Oh, no," Lex stated. "That's definitely Micah and Malik behind him."

"That's what I'm talking about, where are they walking to?"

"I don't know."

"Let's go see what's going on."

Lex barely had time to react because Mya was already halfway out the door.

"I could have you guys arrested for threatening me," Evan yelled. "You don't have a case here."

"I think you may want to lower your voice," Malik said as they walked to a part of the lobby that was somewhat empty.

"I'll tell you what's going to happen," Micah said, done with trying to play nice. "Either you keep my name and Lex's name out of your mouth, or we'll expose you for the embezzling bastard you really are." Micah was trying to calm his nerves, but he had been anxious ever since Malik had told him the information about Evan and Neil Timmons. He was trying to be the bigger person. Be a man about the situation. But his body wasn't listening to his mind, so all Micah wanted to do was knock Evan out cold.

"Your case wouldn't go far," Evan rebuked. "I know people in high places."

"I guarantee we know people in higher places," Shawn said, standing closer to Evan and looking him up and down.

"We'll see," Evan said before he looked past the men to something that had caught his eye. Never one to take their eyes off a target, none of the men turned to see what Evan was looking at.

"You know what," Evan said, shrugging his shoulders, "I can tell you like leftovers so you can have her." He looked straight in Micah's eyes before he continued. "The sex was never that good anyway. And once you get tired of playing with her, you'll throw her away just like I did."

"Be careful, Gilmore," Micah warned as he took two steps toward him.

"What are you going to do?" Evan egged on. "Hit me? Do it! I dare you! You can have that sorry excuse for a woman. I only married her because I felt sorry for her. I—"

Lex's fist connected with Evan's face, catching Evan off guard as well as everyone else. His hand shot up to his chin to cover where she had hit him.

"I know you didn't just hit me b—" Lex's fist connected with Evan's face again, halting whatever he'd been about to say. Her second punch knocked him out cold. Shawn caught Evan before he fell to the ground and sat him in a nearby chair so that it would appear as if he was asleep.

"Oh, man, that felt good," Lex said as she shook her hand in pain.

"What happened to vocalizing your words?" Mya asked Lex with a smirk as she gave her a high five.

"The moment called for hand-to-face contact," Lex said with a laugh.

"What are you doing here?" Micah asked, realizing that she was the trigger that made Evan start talking so much crap.

"I was supposed to be meeting with Evan and I brought Mya with me. He came to my house the other day and had an entire file on you. Although, I'm guessing you already know."

"Malik told me this morning," he said. "But I don't understand why you didn't talk to me."

"Because I wanted to stand up for myself once and for all. Evan had threatened me enough in my lifetime, and I wasn't going to let him dictate who I love or worry you."

Micah had a feeling she'd felt that way, which was why he didn't step in. Lex needed to finally feel in control. But that didn't mean he liked the fact she was going to meet him by herself.

"But Evan is too dangerous for you to deal with on your own."

"I tried to tell her to let you handle it," Mya chimed in, standing off to the side. Micah turned to tell Mya thanks, taking note of the way his brother was glancing at her when he thought she wasn't looking. He would have felt sorry for Malik if he hadn't noticed Mya trying just as hard not to look at him.

"Based off what I heard," Lex said, breaking his observation of his brother and Mya, "I understand that now. And you said something about embezzlement? What did he do?"

"We can talk about all that later," Micah said, picking up her hand and kissing her swollen knuckles. "All I want to do now is take care of your hand and make sure that we're okay."

She smiled as she raised her hand to his cheek. "We're okay," she said, lightly kissing his lips. "I know the type of man you are so I knew there was more to the story than what Evan told me. I just needed some time to myself to figure out how I was going to handle the situation."

"Thanks for believing in me," he said, pulling her

closer. "But please promise me that you will talk to me if you ever have a question about my past, instead of keeping things to yourself."

"Deal," she said as she pulled him closer to her for a kiss. The minute he heard her moan, he deepened their kiss, his tongue frolicking with hers, igniting all his senses in a way only she knew how to do.

The next night, Lex snuggled in Micah's arms on her couch as they watched a romantic comedy on Netflix. Micah had tried to convince her to watch an action movie, but once she told him that she'd had enough action for one holiday, he'd obliged her request to watch a romance.

After the incident with Evan, her and Micah had a long conversation about everything that they'd uncovered. She had already concluded that the situation with Neil had been something that Micah wasn't involved with, but she was glad to know what role Micah had played in the situation.

Ashley Anderson had had a huge crush on Micah in college and had followed him around for months. Although he constantly told her he wasn't interested, she hadn't listened and still tried to pursue him. When Neil Timmons had visited Micah in college, Ashley flirted with him to make Micah jealous. She even went so far as to ask Micah if she could come to his room to see Neil. Micah knew she was trying to make him jealous, but he didn't care, so he agreed.

Once Neil and Ashley started making out in his dorm room, Micah left, having better things to do than watch them make out. He was halfway out his dorm when he realized he forgot his book bag. When he went back to his room, Neil was forcing himself on Ashley and she fought back and begged him to stop. Micah acted quickly on his feet and attacked Neil, knocking him to the ground. His dorm neighbors had heard the screams and had called the police. But by the time the police arrived, Ashley had told the cops that both of them had forced themselves on her and they were both arrested. Micah tried telling the officers he didn't do it, but there was no use.

From what Micah was told, when Ashley's parents arrived, her mom was able to figure out the truth and Ashley finally told the police officers the true story about what had happened. She then apologized to Micah. Her parents removed her from the school and Neil was released because Ashley dropped the charges. By that time, the damage to Micah's reputation on campus was already done and his parents had been notified. The entire time Micah had retold the story, Lex's love for him grew deeper.

"I'll be right back," Micah said, getting up from the couch before returning with his bag.

"I was going to wait for Christmas," he said as he pulled out a red box with a green ribbon tied around it, "but I think tonight is a perfect time to give this to you."

Lex squinted her eyes at him before she untied the ribbon and opened the box. Her eyes softened and her voice briefly caught in her throat.

"Micah, it can't be," she said as her fingers glazed over the delicate item in the box. "How did you find another brooch?"

"After your dad said he found one in Michigan, I figured I would take a chance and have Malik check a few places in the Detroit area. He found this one in a more upscale area while we were in Arkansas. The owner of an antique shop had decided to keep it for herself, but Malik told her the story and she decided that it belonged to you."

"It must have cost so much money," she said.

"It did," he replied. "But she didn't charge anywhere near what I bet she paid for it."

"Wow," Lex said as she twisted the brooch so that the gems and diamonds sparkled in the light. "It's nice to know there are still good people out there."

"It is," he agreed.

"How did you know what the other two brooches looked like?"

"When I was at your parents' house, I asked them if they had a picture of all three brooches and they did."

She leaned in to kiss him before returning her eyes to the brooch. "Having two of the three brooches means the world to me."

"And I'm confident we'll find the third one," Micah said with a smile. She returned his smile, allowing his optimism to flow threw her. Even if they weren't able to locate the third brooch, Lex felt extremely lucky to have a man who cared so much about her happiness.

"I love the man you are Micah Madden," she said, cupping his face in her hands. "I love your strength," she said placing a kiss on his forehead. "I love your loyalty." She placed a kiss on his cheek. "I love your confidence." She placed a kiss on his other cheek. "I love your drive and determination." She kissed his neck. "I love everything about you and being with you makes me a better woman. Thanks for loving me for who I am."

With that, she leaned in for another kiss, this time making sure that it represented all the love and admiration she felt in the depths of her heart.

Epilogue

6 weeks later...

It seemed most of the townspeople of Cranberry Heights were in attendance for the 35th anniversary party of Mason and Cynthia Madden. The look on the couple's faces when they walked into the barn house and realized it wasn't a Founder's Day party, but their anniversary party, had been priceless. Cynthia began shedding happy tears almost immediately, and most of the women at the party had cried right along with her.

Lex glanced around at the beautifully decorated barn and soaked in the feeling of accomplishment. The combination of rustic decor with a vibrant old-world color scheme gave the event a very classy ambiance while maintaining the overall atmosphere of Cranberry Heights. It felt good to be back in Cranberry Heights and she was glad she finally got to meet all of Micah's brothers and cousins. The group had met for dinner in Little Rock a couple days prior so that Mason and Cynthia wouldn't know they were in town. They'd been all too willing to share embarrassing stories about Micah and even though Lex had been the only nonrelative in attendance, she'd felt like she'd grown up with Micah's family.

She got a chill when she thought about how miserable her life would have been had she remained married to Evan. His insolent words no longer affected her and she was done punishing herself for ever being with a man like him. Evan's trial was starting in a few weeks and new victims of his embezzlement were popping up in the news every day. Lex didn't have any sympathy for him and had even learned that he'd had two failed relationships after her and had stolen much more than brooches and pride from the other women. Lex was finally able to put the situation entirely behind her, but she hoped the other women he wronged sued him for all he was worth, even though that wasn't much.

Although Micah and Shawn had originally lost the support of Grant & Parker Inc. after Micah informed them of his prior acquaintance with Neil Timmons, they'd recently called Micah and Shawn to set up a business dinner. They also asked that they bring their significant others, so Lex had prepped Cyd and the two were prepared to support their men and prove to Grant & Parker that M&M Security was a company they could trust.

"Oh, Lex, sweetie," Cynthia said, breaking her thoughts as she pulled her into a warm hug, "Micah told me that Elite Events planned this party. You did such a fantastic job and I absolutely love everything!"

"It was my pleasure," she replied, returning her embrace.

"Come with me," Cynthia said as she linked arms with Lex. "There's something I want to show you."

"Sure," Lex responded. Since returning to Chicago, Lex and Micah's relationship had been on a complete upswing. No matter what she did, she just couldn't seem to get enough of him. Had Micah not been so persistent on having a relationship with her, Lex would have missed out on the love of a lifetime.

"Please wait here," Cynthia told Lex as she unlinked their arms and walked away.

"Um, okay," Lex said, although Cynthia had already dipped through the crowd and was out of earshot.

Lex stood in the middle section of the barn that had been set up for dancing. There were a few groups of people standing near her chatting, but she felt awkward standing there by herself when most of the attendees were sitting at the tables that surrounded the dance floor.

Lex turned around to find out where Cynthia had run off to when suddenly a song by Bruno Mars filled the speakers and one of the groups near her started dancing.

Man they're good, she thought, bopping her head to the song as she watched them dance together in unison. She was so wrapped up in the people who were twirling to the music that she didn't notice ten more people had joined the dance until she felt all eyes on her.

Lex did a 360-degree turn as she whipped her head around the room. *It can't be...*she thought when she realized that she was the only person standing on the dance floor who wasn't dancing. Her heart began beating profusely, and she finally began listening to the upbeat words in the song, which spoke of love, spontaneity and *marriage*.

Lex placed both her hands on her cheeks as she watched the people dance around her, making it unmistakably clear that she was the main attraction. Suddenly, out the corner of her eye, she saw Micah's brothers and cousins make their way onto the dance floor, each one of them swaying to the beat of the music and joining the others in harmony.

Her eyes began filling with tears and she briefly glanced at Cynthia and Mason Madden who were standing on the sidelines wrapped in each other's arms. *Don't cry, Lex...hold it together.* Her heart swelled at the possibility that Micah would go through all this trouble to propose and she wanted to enjoy every second of this precious moment.

Just when she'd calmed her nerves and had gotten her *almost* tears under control, Imani, Cyd and Mya entered the dance floor followed by Daman and Shawn.

"Oh, my goodness," she said aloud as her hand flew to her mouth in astonishment. Never in her entire life had she felt so adored...so cherished...so wanted. She clutched her heart and released the tears she'd been trying to hold in. By the time her parents, Linda and Ethan Turner, had made their way to the dance floor, Lex was an emotional wreck. She wasn't just crying because people who barely knew her were participating in the moment or because people she loved had taken time out their busy lives to be a part of it. She cried because she felt loved...truly and unconditionally loved by Micah Madden.

As the song reached the last couple bars, everyone who was dancing split as they continued moving in a type of soul-train line. Her parents stepped out of the line to escort her in between the two lines of dancers before they joined Micah's parents on the sidelines.

Suddenly, everyone stopped dancing and began clapping to the beat of the music. Lex wiped her tears as she glanced around the crowd, already knowing that Micah was somewhere in the room, based on the way her body was reacting. When he finally came into vision at the front of the dance line, he wasn't moving to the beat as everyone else had been. He was walking purposefully, his eyes locked to hers as he strolled past all the smiling people.

He was wearing black slacks and a deep maroon button-up that matched her burgundy dress perfectly. Even though they'd purposely chosen to dress in similar colors, he looked so different in that moment. So vibrant. And she noticed a small microphone attached to his shirt. She knew what was happening, but she was still nervous, although excitement quickly overtook her nervousness. When he finally reached her, he seized both her hands in his. The DJ turned the music lower and everyone in the dance floor began clapping softer.

"Lexus Tuner," Micah said before he cleared his throat. "When I first met you, I immediately knew that you were the type of woman I could spend the rest of my life with. You understand me, you love me for who I am and, more importantly, you make me strive to be a better person… a better man. You are such an amazing and beautiful woman and I love your strength, your compassion and your willingness to be there for others. But my love for you goes beyond the obvious. I love the faces you make when you get serious or uptight, I adore your clumsiness and the way you make me laugh, too. And I love the crazy words you say to keep yourself from cursing. You may have run into me and fallen the first couple times we met," he said with a chuckle as others joined in the laughter, "but I've been the one falling for you ever since."

He nodded at Shawn, who walked over holding a bright white box. "So, what do you say," Micah said as he got down on one knee and opened a box that contained a gorgeous princess-cut diamond ring sitting on top of a red velvet cupcake. "Will you marry me, Lex?"

Tears filled her eyes and she grinned from ear to ear, still in shock that he'd managed to plan the entire elaborate proposal using a flash mob of their closest family, friends and Cranberry Heights residents. "Of course I'll marry you," she said into the mic loud enough for everyone to hear.

The crowd erupted in applause and the DJ turned the music back up as everyone started dancing to the end of the song. Micah rubbed off a little of the cream cheese frosting that had gotten on the ring before he placed the ring on her finger. He gave her a soft kiss right before the sea of guests came to congratulate them.

"Just so you know," Micah said as he took the red velvet cupcake out of the box and held it to her mouth. "I personally made this cupcake."

She gave him a soft smile. "I can't believe you remembered I love red velvet dessert," she said as she took a bite of the delicious treat.

"This is amazing," she said, savoring the tasty mouthful. She put the dessert back in the box before placing it on a nearby table. "You know what this means."

He laughed as he encircled his arms around her waist. "What does this mean?"

"I've been cooking a lot lately and if you can cook

dessert this well, I think you owe me a few more cooked meals before we solidify this union," she said jokingly.

"Baby, you can have any meal you desire," he said with a laugh as he pulled her even closer to him. "In the meantime, how about you give me what I desire." He glanced down at her lips before licking his own.

She enclosed her arms around his neck. "And what might that be?" she asked, although she had a pretty good idea.

Instead of answering her question, he dipped his head to hers as he captured her lips in the sweetest red velvet kiss.

* * * * *

The first two stories in the *Love in the Limelight* series, where four unstoppable women find fame, fortune and ultimately… true love.

LOVE IN THE LIMELIGHT

New York Times bestselling author

BRENDA JACKSON

&

A.C. ARTHUR

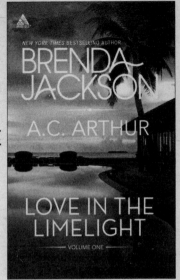

In *Star of His Heart*, Ethan Chambers is Hollywood's most eligible bachelor. But when he meets his costar Rachel Wellesley, he suddenly finds himself thinking twice about staying single.

In *Sing Your Pleasure*, Charlene Quinn has just landed a major contract with L.A.'s hottest record label, working with none other than Akil Hutton. Despite his gruff attitude, she finds herself powerfully attracted to the driven music producer.

Available now wherever books are sold!

KPLIM11631014R

Just in time for the holiday season!

HOT
Christmas
NIGHTS

Fan Favorite Authors
FARRAH ROCHON
TERRA LITTLE
VELVET CARTER

These new novellas offer perfect holiday reading! Travel to Tuscany, Las Vegas and picturesque Bridgehampton with three couples who are about to experience very merry seduction against the perfect backdrops for everlasting love.

"The heat from the two leads practically sets the pages on fire, but it's the believable dialogue and well-defined characters and storyline that make this novel a must-read."
—RT Book Reviews on Farrah Rochon's
A Forever Kind of Love

Available now wherever books are sold!

REQUEST YOUR FREE BOOKS!

2 FREE NOVELS PLUS 2 FREE GIFTS!

KIMANI™ ROMANCE

Love's ultimate destination!

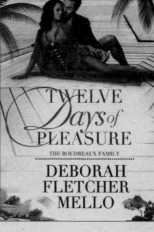

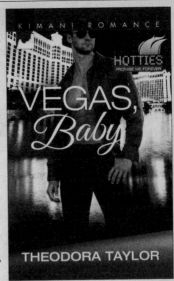